THE HUNTER REBORN
By R. Richardsson

Cover art by; Lars Nielsen

For my wife, who continues to stand beside me in my writing ventures.

Also for C.B., who recognized me at my part time job and later brought in a printed copy of my ebook for a signature.

And for Gabe, who has shown me the error of my ways.

Table of Contents

PROLOGUE

"Excuse me Miss, can you tell me anything about the patient in 103?" His voice was smooth, sensual, and as he spoke, a rather pleasant chill ran down her spine. Before looking up from her work, she moved the pointer on her computer screen to the save icon and clicked.

As her eyes began moving up from her work to meet those of the speaker across from her, her breath caught in her throat. He wore a form fitting black shirt, which was not only decorated with three inverted chevrons on the sleeves, but was also adorned with a badge that identified his precinct by number.

"Ma'am," he asks politely, reminding her that he had a question waiting to be answered.

Her eyes snapped up and for a brief moment she thinks she won't be able to bring herself to reply. His face is chiseled and handsome; offering her a melting smile as he patiently waits for her answer. His oceanic eyes are warm and full of compassion, drawing her further away from what little bit of professionalism she had left.

He runs his right hand up through his thick black hair and clears his throat, glancing down the hall toward the room he had originally asked about.

"I-I'm sorry Sergeant, it's been a long night." Her cheeks are slightly flushed, and as she speaks, she can feel a nervous energy building up within her. "The patient is currently resting comfortably, but has yet to regain consciousness."

He nodded thoughtfully as she confirmed this to him, at the same time reaching down to a small pouch attached to his belt. As she finishes speaking, he moves his left hand across the desk and gently lays it on top of her right, at the same time leaning in until his mouth is a breath away from her right ear.

"If anything changes, please don't hesitate to give me a call," he whispers softly.

The combined effect of his touch and warm breath sends a hot flash roaring through her, nearly causing her to swoon from its sudden rush. As he backs away from her, he lifts his hand and in its place is his

card. He then gives her a smile dangerous enough to
melt her heart, glances down the hallway once more, and
turns to leave.

"Sergeant," she calls out unexpectedly. The sound of
her voice startles her, as it hadn't been her intention
to say anything, and inwardly she chastises herself for
acting like such a timid schoolgirl.

"Yes?"

"Your men DID manage to catch the one responsible for
all this madness, didn't they?" Her voice quivers
fearfully as she speaks and her eyes are like saucers,
openly displaying her unease to him.

He turns to regard her, the remnants of his brilliant
smile still on the edge of his expression.

"We have a suspect in custody, yes," he offers.

"So is it true," she asks.

"I'm sorry?"

"You know… Is it true that he's crazy? I mean, I
heard that he was carrying a black bag with all sorts of
crazy things in it."

The smile vanished completely from his expression as
a dark cloud seems to come over it. His brow furrows
together, and in the moment before he next speaks, his
lips tighten into a thin white line.

"What have you heard," he asked tonelessly, "…and
from whom did you hear it?"

Immediately her heart sank to the lowest pits of her
stomach and she felt nauseous at the thought that this
beautiful creature was angry with her.

"O-only that he had this black bag and in it were
these little books written in some other language," she
answered carefully. In truth, she had heard about a
couple other things which had been found in that bag,
but at this point she only wanted back the smiling
Adonis that had stood before her just moments ago.

Seconds stretched into minutes as he considered her
answer. To her relief, the look of anger finally faded
from his expression.

"I'm sorry," he offered with a hint of the smile he
had earlier given to her. "This is a sensitive matter
that we're dealing with. It's imperative that nothing

gets out to the public before we've had a chance to go over all of the details."

The rising panic which had been building up inside of her melted away as he once again turned those deep blue eyes into hers. Reaching once more across the desk, the smile having returned to full strength, he once again placed his hand over hers before speaking.

"I didn't catch your name."

"It's Natalie. Natalie Hendrick."

"It's a pleasure to meet you Natalie. You may call me, Michael."

THE COMING DAWN

He sits on the edge of the bunk, completely enveloped in darkness, with his legs spread slightly and elbows resting just behind his knees. His head is facing the floor, resting into his upturned palms, and the only sound in the room is the occasional tear after it rolls off the end of his nose and splashes against the tiled floor.

There is very little to remind him of how he arrived in his cell, with most of his memories having fled the onslaught of his grief long ago, and even with his eyes closed he can still see her dying visage floating before him. No matter how hard he tries not to, he can still smell the soft hint of Scotch on her breath. She had continued to look into his eyes lovingly, even after her death, and he could still feel her gentle touch against his cheek.

He slid his hand to where she had last touched him and once again felt the bloody print she had left on his face. He recoiled in horror. His mind created a new image of his lost friend, one which looked up into his eyes as if to blame him for what had happened to her.

"How could you have let this happen to me Jooohn," the apparition implored of him. Blood gushed from her mouth, gurgling as she spoke, and it poured in rivers from the wounds in her chest and leg onto the floor below.

"I'm dead because of you!"

He croaked feebly, unable to answer as he swatted at the ghost before him. Its lips curl upward into a hideous smile, exposing sharp canines that slowly lengthen out of its mouth.

"Look at what you've done to me! Aren't I jussst the prettiessst thing? Come on Jooohn, come give me a kisss!"

He flinches, throwing his arms in front of his eyes while trying to fend off the evil thoughts assailing him. The specter cackled, taunting him with its rictus grin, and suddenly the pain is just too much for him to bear. From deep inside of him a low moan begins to emanate, full of pain and outrage as he languished over the ones he had so recently lost. The sound arose from within the depths of his soul, and as it increased in momentum, so too does it increase in volume until he is unable to contain it any longer.

His head tilts back as he releases a wail so full inner torment that the power alone sent the vermin scattering into every nook and cranny to escape its wrath. The sound gushed from him like a waterfall, slipping around the cracks of the door and into the hall on the other side. It followed the walls, passing by cells just like the one he was sitting in, into a central area occupied by one larger holding cell.

It spread into the holding cell, weaving around the bars and pummeling the eardrums of a drunk sleeping on one of the many benches there-in. Awakened by the terrifying noise, and still feeling the effects of the previous night's bender, he falls from the bench and crawls hurriedly over to the darkest corner he can find, curling into a ball and babbling incoherently to himself. The sound travels quickly up a nearby stairwell, and around the door at the top, into the room beyond.

The room has several desks pushed against one another in the center allowing for each officer to face each other while they work, and it's at two such desks that the anguished wail ends its journey.

Nearest the stairwell, one officer is leaning back in his chair, thumbing through the newest equipment catalogue while his partner is finishing up some paperwork across from him. The sound startles him so much that he jumps to his feet, his hand immediately going to his sidearm.

Across from him, his partner loses his balance and crashes to the floor.

"Jesus-Jumped-Up-Christ," he exclaims as he claws his way back to this feet. "What the hell is THAT?!"

"I think it's that prisoner they brought in from the James Street Massacre, at the old clothing store. Hey, I got an idea, why don't you go find out," the first cop suggests as he takes his hand off of his holster and sits back down behind his desk.

"You're fucking kidding right? Did you not just hear that shit?"

"Yeah, I sure did just hear that shit, Officer Vargas. Are you trying to tell me you're afraid of a little noise that may or may not be coming from a prisoner locked in solitary?"

Vargas only looked across their desks, glaring at his partner as he pushed his chair beneath his own before walking to the stairs leading down to containment.

"You're a real dick, you know that?"

"And you're out of line," the other returns as he tosses a set of keys to him. "Here, take these with you. They might be helpful."

"Yeah, yeah," Vargas muttered as he turns away.

He approaches the door with trepidation. Even though the sound had since faded and the office had returned to its previous state of silence, his nerves were still sensitive toward anything else that might come unexpected.

Upon reaching the door, he lifts the key ring and begins sorting through the keys until he finds the one that will turn the lock.

The key rattled in the lock as he turns it, and after a moment of fumbling, clicks open. His partner had stopped working on his reports long enough to watch him open the door, and when he turned to face him, gives an exaggerated smile as he waves. Vargas flipped a middle finger in return before turning back and entering the stairwell.

After pulling the door shut behind him, he turned around and carefully walked down the stairs, thirteen in all. As he got closer to the bottom he could hear the sound of someone softly whimpering nearby. It took a moment of searching, something he never thought that he'd have to do in the cell where they kept the lesser offenders, but he managed to find the drunk who had been earlier brought in on a DUI.

He was curled in a fetal position between the metal toilet and the far wall, his arms around his knees, rocking gently back and forth.

"Hey," he called out softly. "What's going on in there?"

3

"Pleash," the other whined pitifully in response. "Pleash make it shtop!"

Just as he was about to yell at the frightened man, a baritone voice poured into the corridor, bouncing off of the walls and surrounding them. It originated from the other prisoner's cell, an indecipherable chanting which was low and unlike anything he had ever heard. Vargas stepped back from the holding area, momentarily startled, and glanced furtively toward the solitary confinement area. At his feet, a soft metallic jingle went unnoticed.

"Oh god, I shwear I'll never drink again if you jusht get me the hell out of here," the man in the holding area babbled fearfully.

The voice continued to build in cadence and volume, much like it had done with the anguished wail moments before, only this time it was reciting word after word in a language unknown to him. His palms suddenly began to sweat as he squints, attempting to peer into the darkness of what he called *The Bad Stretch*; forty straight feet of hallway, on either side of which were four reinforced rooms used for solitary confinement.

His heart drummed in his chest as suddenly from behind, and a little ways above him, there came a dull thumping. The drunk, who had returned to the shadows between the wall and the toilet, suddenly shrieked in terror. The combination of both caused him to involuntarily stumble backwards, first to get away from the thumping noise above, and then to get the HELL away from the shrieking man in front of him. His left foot slipped out from beneath him as it skidded on something metallic, causing it to slide out from under him. The result was him tumbling to a heap on the ground, his legs forming a 'V' before him with his hands supporting him from behind.

The voice rose in volume as it continued to chant in its strange dialect. Parallel to its ascension, his fear continued to rise as well. One by one the dim emergency bulbs down *The Bad Stretch* exploded, bringing the darkness ever closer to the main holding area, until only the light above him was all that remained.

4

His eyes remain frozen in the direction the chanting was originating and he unconsciously scooted himself backward, closer to the wall. As the terror welled up from within, all other sounds faded into the background. The steady thumping from the top of the stairs is replaced by the thudding of his own heart heavily beating in his chest.

The voice of the man in solitary continued to rise in volume, its words filling with an electric power that he can feel crawling over his skin like a thousand tiny fingers. He doesn't realize it but he has begun to shriek, each deep breath producing a sound worthy of any 'B' movie scream queen.

Inside the holding cell, the solitary occupant has also succumbed to the same feelings of terror Vargas is experiencing. The moment that the officer fell to the floor and the lights began to burst, he darted to the bars nearest the hallway. His hands are wrapped around the bars directly in front of each of his shoulders, gripping onto them so tightly that his knuckles had become white from the strain. He pressed his head forward, trying to squeeze it through in an attempt to better make himself heard over the cacophony of words around him, and he began to scream his own song of fright toward the stairwell.

Amidst the shrieks and the pleas that continued to go unanswered, the voice continued to march along the cadence of its speech. It reverberated off of the walls, booming its message, and a sickly yellow glow pierced the darkness beyond the cell from which the voice was speaking. There were two sources to this light, small and focused as if the speaker were holding two pen lights.

However, unlike the light which comes from a flashlight, these two beams did not reach the other side of the hall. Just as sickly as their color was their strength. As the length of each beam seemed to pulse, reaching outward with the force of the words being spoken, they also drew quickly back into the cell in the silence between them.

And then, just as suddenly as it had begun, the voice fell silent. The golden beams of light fled into the

cell and the hallway down *The Bad Stretch* was gone from
sight as the darkness rushed in to cover it once more.

An unnatural calm crept over the containment area,
washing over the two men where were still consumed by
feelings they couldn't control. Respectively, Vargas
and the drunk eventually become silent; the former
looking up into the frightened eyes of the latter, whose
face was still pressed between the bars as far as he
could get it.

"Pleash mishter. For the love of God, pleash let me
out?"

At that moment the fluorescent bulb over the holding
area exploded, plunging the cell into darkness behind
him, and there came a bubbling sound from the corner
where he had recently cowered. It was a sound not
unlike boiling water, only there was something more
sinister underlying it. Soft, almost unnoticeable,
beneath the bubbling sound of water was something one
would expect to hear when letting the air out of a tire.

"Fuuuck…this," Vargas suddenly croaked when, in the
darkness behind the other came the sound of something
wet plopping onto the concrete. He half turned, clawing
at the wall as pulled his legs under him in an attempt
to return to his feet.

The drunk suddenly reached through the bars and
latched onto his tie, pulling him close enough that
Vargas could smell the alcohol on his breath.

"GET ME OUT OF HERE," he screeched at him.

There was no reasoning left in Vargas. Nothing the
man could say would at this point be logical enough to
keep him down here any longer. There was nothing in his
seven years on the force that could even come close to
preparing him for what was happening down here.

The sound of boiling water churned more urgently in
the darkness and there were several more wet splats
against the concrete.

Vargas jerked mechanically, frantically batting at
the hands of the person keeping him from getting as far
away from here as possible. There was a brief struggle
as each man, whose blood now flowed with adrenaline born
of terror, fought two separate battles; one to get away
from his captor and flee from this seemingly haunted

basement, and the other to keep him rooted until he was
set free, that they might both escape.

From behind the only locked door in solitary, the
prisoner's voice suddenly spoke with an intense sadness.

"It is too late. He has come."

Their struggle ceased when the prisoner's voice stole
from the darkness and each had turned toward it to
listen to what it had to say. At the moment that he
finished speaking, so too did the sounds in the darkness
of the holding cell cease as well.

"…pleash…"

The drunk had unknowingly loosened his grip on Vargas
when the other prisoner had spoken, allowing enough
slack that the latter could now slip out of his reach.

"Pleash," he begged for the second time, one hand
reaching pitifully outward. His fingers were stretched
out and he tried to force as much of his shoulder
through the bars as possible to help shorten the
distance between them, but there wasn't going to be much
relief this time. Vargas was too far away and the bars
were made specifically for this purpose.

As Vargas stepped into the line of sight of those on
the other side of the small window in the door above,
the thumping renewed as his partner pounded on it from
the other side.

"…open the door!"

Vargas had just enough time to reflect on how he
could barely hear his partner. He thought of when he
was on the other side and he had heard the prisoner in
solitary as if he had been right next to him, when
suddenly a pair of glowing eyes appeared in the darkness
of the holding cell.

They were behind the poor man reaching out to him,
who continued begging to be let out of the cell and who
was also yet unaware of the danger behind him. They
hovered a full foot over his head and seemed to be
staring deep into Vargas's terror-filled soul.

From the top of the stairs, he could hear his name
being called by his partner, but he couldn't find the
strength to move. His eyes were locked onto the two
amber colored orbs floating behind the man in front of
him. They seemed to sway gently back and forth and he

7

found himself quickly enthralled by their hypnotic dance.

As he continued to stare into the eyes before him, marveling at their color and dismissing their slit pupils as being effects caused by contacts, it never occurred to Vargas to question who the eyes belonged to. In fact, from that moment on, nothing ever occurred to him again. He now belonged to the one with the amber colored eyes.

As frightened as he was, the man in the holding area had enough sense left to realize that something else in the cell behind him. He had begun to cry when the officer slid out of his grasp and his whole body to tremble as he watched the muscles in the other's face grow slack.

Slowly, he pulled his hand back through the bars and turned until his back was against them. At first, he wasn't able to see a thing. The darkness was almost complete near the back of the cell, the light from the bottom of the stairwell was unable to even touch it, but he could just make out a slender form in the shadows before him. He slowly followed its shape upward until he found what the cop had been staring at.

The silence would once again be broken, but this time it was by a sound that the drunk had never heard before. It was also the last sound that he would ever know. Near the ground, and only a few feet in front of him, the silence fled for the final time before a loud rattling that was not unlike the sound of several bones clacking together. His hands snapped out to either side of him, grabbing onto the bars behind him, as a serpentine head suddenly darted out of the darkness and bit his head off. His last thoughts were of how the snake, though its scales were black with red highlights, had looked almost human. As his eyes began to close for the final eternal slumber he was now rapidly approaching, he saw the mouth of the snake closing around his gushing neck.

A soft groan slipped past his lips as he began to regain consciousness. His entire body ached. It felt like he had been running a marathon, but he knew better. In his entire life, he had never run further than from his living room to his bathroom after eating something which hadn't agreed with him.

"*What I wouldn't give to be back on my recliner,*" he thought miserably.

He was lying on his stomach. There was no telling how long he had been there, aside from the intense feeling of pain coursing through his arms and legs. While the latter seemed to be unfettered, his arms were restrained behind him and had, at some point, fallen asleep. He began to carefully adjust his weight, so as to not cause any further pain in his arms, and rolled to his side.

Though his actions were small, the resulting effect was huge. Blood began to flow down into his long dormant arms, which were now lower than his heart, and thus reawakening his sleeping appendages. The pain was more than he could bear, causing him to cry out as it began rolling over him in waves.

As he battled to revitalize himself, a distant question about how much time had passed skirted the edge of his thoughts. It wasn't much, but it was enough to help distract him from the intense sensations in his arms. He began to work his wrists back and forth, trying to create enough slack through which to free one of his hands. It was no easy task, and his thoughts weren't enough to completely distract him from the pain, but he eventually managed to slip out of his bonds. He sighed with relief as he moved his hands in front of him, taking turns massaging each for several minutes while trying to get his bearings.

He quickly learned that there was no way for him to identify his surroundings. He is surrounded in an endless sea of darkness. He blinked his eyes several times, hoping to adjust his vision enough to determine

where he was, but even his night eyes couldn't focus
enough to see.

"John," he asked softly. "John, are you there?"

As he speaks, something puffs away from his face. At
first it doesn't register to him its nature, until he
recognizes its odor. He is lying on sawdust!

He waited for a moment before again calling out to
his friend, and again there was no reply.

"Chloe?"

His attempts to raise her prove as fruitless as the
first two and he surmised that they must either be
unable to answer, or something worse had befallen them.

He tried to remember the last thing that had
happened, but the memory danced just out of reach. He
knew that there had been something important that they
had been doing…

"The Clothing Store," he gasped.

He had been standing just inside the door, while to
the right and in front of him, Chloe had been in the
midst of a fierce struggle with three of the albino's
henchmen. John had been further to the left. He had
just sheathed the silver blade with the bell shaped
guard from his left hand, while his right had been
reaching down to draw *Jessie* from her holster. Several
feet in front of him stood the vampire they had all come
to slay; the monster Draegan. The same creature which
had taken the sister after whom John had named his
weapon and whom had torn Brody to pieces at the rest-
stop just hours before.

"What the hell was that," Chloe screams.

*"And lo shall evil make known its presence, and the
earth shall tremble," John answers.*

"Quinn?"

"I—is it t—time John?"

"Yes my friend. You know what to do."

*With fingers that felt like they no longer belonged
to him, Quinn reaches into his pocket and took hold of…*

"M—my notebook!"

His pains forgotten for the moment, he reached into
his breast pocket to see if it was there. He slipped

10

his fingers, which were now tingling at every slight movement, into his pocket hoping to find the only tool he had been able to use.

Nothing…

He must have dropped it after… After…

"*W-what was it t-that I had been doing,*" he asked quietly.

There was a dull ache in the back of his head; one which he hadn't noticed before but was now sure had been there all along. Slowly, afraid of the answer he knew he was going to find, he began moving his right hand up towards his face. Without removing his fingertips from his skin, he continues upwards, passing lightly over his neck before moving around to his back. Reaching the back of his neck confirms his suspicions when his fingers suddenly touch something that's crusty and flakey at his touch; dried blood. There's no doubt in his mind that he had been attacked from behind!

A wave of nausea passes over him, replacing the faint tingling sensation as blood rushes back into his limbs, and he begins to cry. Never before has he felt as utterly alone as he does at this very moment. As the tears pour down his cheeks, he pulls his legs up to his chest and for the next half hour he mourns for his past, for his friends, and for his lost self.

After the grief had run its course, and after he had finally regained complete feeling in his limbs, he began to explore his enclosed surroundings. The first thing he discovered was that he was lying atop a pile of sawdust. The scent of pine permeated most of his senses, beneath which he could detect his own fear, and that was of no help to him.

Slowly, he stretches his right arm out in front of him. Before he is able to completely straighten it, however, he met with firm resistance. At first he is confused. The material of the wall was neither warm nor cool, but is rough to the touch. He brushes his fingers lightly over the material until something suddenly pricked his index finger.

"Wood," he muttered softly. "M-most likely a c-crate of s-some k-kind."

He had never been one to think aloud, but in the darkness and without his notebook, the sound of his voice helped soothe him. A few more minutes of searching confirm his suspicions. He was sealed inside a wooden box that only gave him just enough room to lie down, with his knees bent, or to sit with his chin against his chest. Not enough room for comfort, but then again, it was very likely that this feature wasn't in the original designs.

He sat with his back to one wall, slumped so that he didn't have to have his head bent, and he did something that he hadn't been able to think of doing until now; he listened. There were sounds outside of his prison, most were indecipherable, but he could pick out the occasional soft creaking. It was rhythmic and soothing in its own way, but he was more concerned about the gentle swaying below him.

As he contemplated the implications of his discovery, he heard the sound of approaching footsteps. They were muffled, and they didn't come to where he was being held captive, but he counted at least two sets of feet making the noise.

"How long before we set sail. I'm ready to get the hell out of this place."

The first speaker's voice was high pitched and nasally. Small squeaks in the tone indicated that he was probably in his teens.

"It should be another week."

The second speaker's voice was deeper, and not quite as nasally as the first's. The footsteps came closer to his prison before the baritone voice spoke again.

"This is the cargo that the boss wants you to care for. Make sure when you open that hatch," there is a brief pause, "that you don't remove this pin. Got it?"

"Y-yeah. But, what happens, if say, that were to happen?"

"If you know what's good for you, it won't."

There is another pause, followed by the sound of footsteps retreating as the two walked away.

"H-how often do I, you know?"

"Once a day," Baritone answers. "The boss only wants this one alive. Nothing else matters beyond that."

12

The voices faded away and he is once again left with only his thoughts to comfort him.

"*The Boss*?"

He chuckled softly to himself at the thought of having been kidnapped by Bruce Springsteen, but the moment of hilarity quickly passes. He was in trouble, he knew that, and if he didn't find a way to get out of this prison and to his friends, there would be very little hope of him seeing the light of day again.

"W-what would John do," he asked quietly.

If only he could see! If he had at least enough light by which to take in his surroundings, he could more easily formulate a plan to escape.

"I w-wonder…"

An idea had taken root as he frantically searched through his pockets. He already knew that his notebook was no longer in his breast pocket, but there might be a chance that they hadn't thoroughly searched him. If this was the case, then he could use…

"M-my phone!"

His left hand closed around the plastic shell of his cell phone and he sobbed in relief as he removed it from his pocket.

"Please," he muttered as he pressed in the screen lock button.

The screen suddenly flared to life. He cringed, nearly dropping the phone when the light was brighter than he had expected, and squeezed his eyes tightly shut. Raising his right hand to his face, he frantically rubbed his eyes until they re-adjusted to the brightness of the light.

After what felt like an eternity his vision began to clear, and by squinting his eyes together he is just able to read the information on the screen; there was only one bar left on the battery. Worse yet, there was no signal.

His shoulders slumped in defeat.

"D-damn it John! What d-do I do n-now?"

In a move more suited to the recently deceased Brody, he curled the fingers of his right hand into a tight ball and lashed out at the wall in front of him. There wasn't much room to get in a full swing, which is good

13

because he might have broken his hand if there had been, but the resulting pain is still more than he had been prepared to handle.

"*Hit it again, little buddy.*"

"Brody?"

He had been holding his hand tightly to his chest, rocking back and forth when the ghostly voice had spoken. He answered partly to ask if that's who it was and partly out of shock, but there was no answer.

"I-I can't," he cried. "It h-hurts too m-much!"

His voice trembled as he fought to hold himself together and he continued to hold his injured hand against his chest. Several more minutes passed before he accepted that there wouldn't be anything further from his lost companion.

Steeling himself for the next blow, he lifted his hand and threw another hard punch. This time there WAS a sharp crack and waves of pain shot up his arm after the impact, but he felt something give! It wasn't much, and thankfully it wasn't him, but it was going to take a lot more pressure before the board broke loose enough to completely knock out. There shined the faintest ray of hope that he was going to get out of this yet.

Muttering a silent "Thank you" to his friend for egging him on from beyond the grave, he began wailing away. Blow after blow rained down upon the wood. Tears are streaming down his face from the pain, but he doesn't allow himself to stop. If this was the beginning of a way out, he had to work through it. He had to get to his friends before something happened to them!

Finally, the board popped loose on the right side. Up on his knees, he places both hands against it and leans in with his full weight. Within seconds, it falls free from the crate with a loud clatter. Instinctively, he scurries against the far side of his cramped prison, preparing for the worst. Several minutes pass, however, and nobody comes to inspect the noise. Cautiously, he approached the newly created portal to the outside and peers through.

From what he can tell, he is in a large storage area. There isn't much light to see by, but he can just make out several shadowy structures that could be shelves, such as the same type he remembered seeing in the back end of *The Clothing Store*. With his face pressed against the new opening, his senses are assaulted by a very strong, pungent scent of death. With a frown, he lifts his shirt up over his nose before looking back into the room outside.

There was no mistaking that he was above the ground. He was just high enough that there was no doubt his captors had been eye level with his prison. The darkness is pushed back when suddenly a beam of light falls from the ceiling. A quick glance confirms the skylight through which the pale moonlight is falling, but more to his interest is the ground below.

If it were a possibility outside of his mind's eye, at that moment he would have heard the sound of his heart splashing into his stomach, as below him he recognizes a scene that had only been described to him several days earlier.

There is a small clearing amidst several metal storage shelves, the kind meant for holding heavy freight, in which he can see a small desk, a work table and an area which looks like it might have once been used as a break area for those who worked here. Across the desk is the decaying body of a man dressed in overalls. It looked like he had at one time been moved post-mortem, as he has been rolled to his side from a dried pool of blood that had likely formed from the gaping hole in his neck. Several other bodies lie in various states around the room, including one which he can only see the legs sticking out from beneath a pile of crates, just opposite of where he was being held.

His stomach lurched and for the second time in minutes, he falls away from the opening. Only, this time he quickly turns as the final contents of his last meal rushed out and splashed against the corner he had positioned himself in. Once finished, he scoops some of the sawdust up and covers the mess.

"G-god help m-me," he manages to choke out.

"There is no God little man," a voice suddenly speaks from the outside. A terrified yawp erupts from his lips, high pitched, and punctuated by a mousy squeak.

15

"He died a bitter old man, wrapped in the tattered remains of his shawl while sitting before the remnants of a burnt out fire. He died with a curse on his lips, damning the creation of your species. HE died with the regret of having created his angels, one whom would love HIM too much and thus make our kind possible."

Despite his terror, he crawled the short distance to the opening he had just made. His very being screamed against his action, as there was absolutely no reason to why he needed to look upon the face of the mysterious speaker. So why then was he continuing towards the sound?

"For centuries we have hidden in the shadows. We have abided by laws created by our masters to protect us from your kind. We've watched helplessly as you intruded into our barrows and murdered our children. You've destroyed our homes so that you could make your own. It's always so important for you to expand, but to what end? After a few years, you abandon the things you create, leaving them to rot."

The speaker stood just on the other side of the moonlight. It was difficult to make out any details, but what manifested was tall and slender and leaned on a cane-like object as it spoke.

"Take this warehouse, for instance. We were perfectly content here, minding our own business, when your friend decided to drop in on us. With his 'visit', he created *this*."

The figure lifted its arms, holding them out for emphasis. Looking at it sparked a brief hint of recognition, but in his state, he wasn't able to grasp onto it before it fled once more into the depths of his mind.

"This, chaos, was created when he killed several of my most dutiful workers. And for what? Just as your kind do with your cities, he left this behind to become the maggot infested cesspool that it is."

The voice was inexplicably angry. Worse still was the sound of its tone, increasing in pitch and volume as it rattled on. Once again he grasps at something familiar about the shape below, only to sigh in frustration when it doesn't come to him.

"It's not like it was a complete loss. You see, this is where our kind comes in. We're the balance in this chaos that you create, the Yang to your Yin. Without us, your kind would have long since destroyed this world by way of your sloppy negligence!"

The voice cackles softly before continuing.

"It isn't going to be long before we have everything we need! And you, my little friend, you are the key! By the time we're through with you, we'll know EVERYTHING about that cursed creature; Van Helsing."

The voice snarled as the last of its words were spoken, and as he watched in horror, the figure stepped fully into the moonlight. He cried out in dismay when he recognized the albino despite the fact that the right side of his face was a barely recognizable mass of scar-tissue. His sanity slipped as something more indescribable began to happen below.

As the moonlight bathed the man's face, it quickly began to swell. The sickening sound of cracking bones filled the room as his face elongated, forming a long canine snout. White hair burst forth from the flesh on the left side of his face, while the right remained bald. His left ear elongated, while the right only partially formed, also like his face, without hair and covered in scar tissue.

The creature fell forward, the rest of its body completing the transformation, sans the right front leg below the knee, as well as patches of fur on that side of the body.

The transformation was quick, taking only a few seconds to complete, and when it was done he looked down in horror at what had to be the biggest jackal he had ever seen. Appearing much like its human form, its non-damaged areas are completely covered by white fur and its eyes were pinkish in hue.

The lycanthrope lifted its head and emitted a roar that was very much like a lion's; deep and powerful. The walls of his prison rumbled from its strength and his ears throbbed painfully. His mouth opened in his terror and he screamed breathlessly, his hands covering his ears. The last thing he saw before his consciousness retreated back into the darkness was the

17

jackal approaching the body slumped over the desk. A
long tongue had slipped out of the side of its mouth as
it began licking its lips in anticipation, spilling
small droplets of drool onto the dried pool of blood
below.

III

WELCOME TO THE A.S.P.D.

Known as "Jonesy" by his coworkers, Officer Lachlan Jones was the shining star of their unit. He had served in the precinct for the past two decades, during which time he had brought hundreds of criminals to justice.

He had seen it all; from petty theft to murder, and everything else in between. During his tenure, he had been shot twice in the line of duty. The first time was by a kid who had stolen a car radio. The bullet had grazed his neck and had it been an inch more to the right, his career would have ended there.

The second bullet had been more serious. He hadn't been wearing his vest on a day when he was answering a routine call to a domestic disturbance at the Drue residence, the home of a couple well known for their physicality when it came to their arguments. Unbeknownst to him, this time would be much different than any previous visit, for Mrs. Drue had grown tired of her husband's cheating ways and had decided that she was going to kill him.

By the time Jonesy had arrived, the deed had been done. She was standing over the body of her husband with a smoking pistol in her hand. Tears were streaming down her bloody face, the same face which Mr. Drue had worked over moments before his demise.

"Ma'am" he barked as he unsnapped the safety strap over his sidearm. "I'm going to have to ask you to dr-"

He never finished the sentence. As if waking from a dream, she raised the gun and fired. The bullet slammed into his chest, puncturing his right lung and sending him spinning to the floor. He had landed on his stomach, coughing up thick clots of blood and struggling to draw in air. He was fighting to pull his firearm free when she put the barrel beneath her chin and fired one last time.

Since that night, the majority of his work took place at the station. His duties included the overseeing and filing of reports turned in by his coworkers, answering phones as needed, placing and removing incoming prisoners into their cells, and occasionally working the

evidence room. On a smaller scale, he worked with any
rookie or new transfer until they were settled in, and
he ran the gun range on the weekends.

Unlike most of the other officers his age, Jonesy
still maintained the semblance of youth. While his
raven colored hair now had more of a salt and pepper
look to it, and there were a few more wrinkles around
his eyes, he could easily pass for someone ten years
younger.

Running a desk hadn't been unkind to him by any
means. While most would have given up on themselves log
ago, he continued to work hard each day in the gym. As
a result, he had as much stamina (if not more), as his
coworkers.

On a daily basis, they would give him grief about his
position behind the desk. They knew as well as he did
that he should be out on the beat, but it was his choice
to work the books. He had never forgiven himself for
what had happened in the Drue residence. It was those
kinds of mistakes that got people killed, and if it
hadn't been him getting shot that day, it could have
been his partner.

There have never been any hard feelings in the
office. Everyone had the utmost respect for him. Aside
from a select few, most of those now on the force had
been trained by Jonesy to some degree. Everyone had, at
one time or another spent some time on the range with
him and was a better marksman for it. His dedication to
the books helped keep out all errors and had saved their
butts on several occasions. They may occasionally give
him some 'shit', but not only was it half-hearted at
best; he always took the ribbing like a champ.

Occasionally he would play along and dish it back out
to them, but for the most part he took his job very
seriously. This was especially true while he was
working on their reports or while in the evidence room.
He believed that these two areas were the heart and soul
of their job, whereas working on the beat was the body.
If the utmost attention wasn't poured into making sure
that the reports were properly filled out and filed, or
that the evidence was categorized and placed where it
belonged, he would work overtime until it was.

"If we aren't paying the same critical eye to our paperwork as we do to the perps, then what the hell's it all for?"

This, or some variation of it, was something his coworkers had gotten used to hearing him to say over the years, and all had learned to stop questioning him over it.

He didn't dislike his work by any means. Where many have come and gone because they didn't want to work a desk, he gladly embraced it. There was never any thought of anyone abusing his willingness to work on the papers, nor had there been many who abused him in this manner. It was simply an accepted part of the well-oiled machine that was the All Saints Police Department. While he was essentially the heart and soul of the station, the officers able to work the beat were the living embodiment of it.

Because of his work, they were able to run their beats longer and were only at their desks long enough to write their initial reports. This year had seen an unusual rise in crime, however, and the amount of paperwork that needed finished was also rising. There were at least three people in the tank at all times, up to a maximum capacity of fifteen, and very rarely did they need to use any of the solitary rooms down the hall from main lockup.

On the night that the A.S.P.D. got their first serial killer, there had only been one person in the holding area; a local drunk by the name of Ronnie Winters. Ronnie had been a regular ever since finding his friends torn apart in the old *Moving and Storage* warehouse. It had been cold that night and whenever the weather was especially bad, such as it was that night, there they would meet to share drinks over a roaring barrel fire.

Like most nights, he had come into the front entrance and sat in the waiting area. Jonesy was going over the report on a DUI from the night before and hadn't seen him enter. His partner, James Vargas, had just stepped out of the locker room and was buttoning up his uniform when the phone rang. Jonesy quickly picked up the receiver, listened carefully to the speaker on the other end before replacing it back in its cradle.

"That was the Captain. She wants us to keep a close eye on our newest guest."

Vargas raised an eyebrow as he strapped on his gun.

"What, exactly, does she suggest? Should we go down and play a round of cards with him?"

"No, dumbass. Turn on the camera. We'll check it every fifteen minutes or so. "

Vargas sighed, rolling his eyes as he shook his head back and forth in exasperation.

"I don't get it. Why was I called in on this one? I mean seriously, we have the guy in solitary. You and I both know that he's not getting out of there unless one of us lets him out."

This time it was Jonesy who shook his head.

"I'm guessing it's real bad down there. She said something about dozens of bodies, with only one possible survivor. I don't know much else…"

Vargas looked over his partner's shoulder and noticed Ronnie lying across several chairs in the waiting area up front.

"God damnit, what's that bum doing here? This ain't the Motel 6!"

Jonesy turned and looked over his shoulder, noticing their regular patron for the first time.

"Take it easy James. He's been through a lot, and I'd like to think that by getting him out of the cold that we're helping him in some small way or another."

His partner only sighed and walked across the office to where Ronnie was now snoring.

"Come on you old drunk," he barked, "let's get you downstairs."

Ronnie jerked, startled from his slumber and nearly falling off of the chairs as he tried to sit up.

"..uh? Shkip? Ish dat you?"

Then, as he suddenly remembered where he was, his shoulders slumped.

"Come on now," Vargas said while grabbing his right arm.

Ronnie's chest hitched as he began to sob, and Vargas directed him toward the stairs leading to the holding area. They only stopped once as Vargas grabbed the key-ring from his partner and within moments they were at the bottom of the stairs.

"I'm shorry," Ronnie uttered pitifully as they stepped into the empty holding area.

"Yeah, yeah. Shut up and get your ass in there."

Vargas shoved him into the cell and locked the door, watching in amusement as the drunk stumbled over to the bench nearest the toilet. As he turned to leave, he cast a quick glance down the hall to the cell where their other guest was being kept. Not seeing anything of interest, he made his way back to the top of the stairs, shut off all but the lights they kept on at night, and locked the door behind him.

"Why do you do that," Jonesy asked; his eyes still down on the report he was currently working on.

"What? I'm just kidding around is all…"

"He didn't do anything to you, first of all. He's just an old drunk with nowhere left to turn. Second of all, you are sworn to *Protect* and *Serve* the public, Officer Vargas. Not this shit you've been pulling lately."

Vargas smirked as he sat in his chair across from his partner and tossed the key-ring over to his desk.

"One of these days that's going to come back and bite you in the ass. You know that, don't you?"

"Jonesy," Vargas sighed, "what difference does it make if I rough up one of these scumbags? If it isn't a drunk looking for a free ride, it's a murderer, or worse. Who cares if I smack these assholes around? Whose word is anyone going to believe, mine or theirs?"

Jonesy, who had calmly continued to work since the beginning of this discussion, laid down his pen, and slowly removed his reading glasses, before looking up at his partner.

"Listen here, you little prick. Let's get something straight, right…now! I will not tolerate this kind of behavior on my shift, not from you or anyone else on the force. Now, if you want to rough some people up in your spare time, that's your prerogative. But when you're wearing that shield, Sir, you are going to damn well *Uphold* the law, *Serve* the public and *Protect* the innocent!"

All of this came out of his mouth calmly. His voice never raised in volume once as he spoke, and his words carried the strong sense of authority behind them.

"Do we have an understanding, partner? Or do I need to have a talk with the Captain when she gets back?"

Vargas, who had been momentarily stunned by his words, only nodded in compliance.

"Good. Now keep an eye on the monitor and make sure nothing happens down there. By the time I finish these reports, they'll be coming back in from the crime scene, and then we can get briefed on what's going on out there."

Jonesy put his reading glasses back on and within seconds was back into his work. His partner, left with much to think about, flipped open his laptop and turned on the camera overlooking *The Bad Stretch*. It was dark inside, with only the emergency lights on, but he could make out all of the cells and the door to the holding area.

"How's it look down there," Jonesy asked. His spoke to him as if nothing had happened.

"Quiet," came his only response.

Jonesy grunted, apparently satisfied with the simple answer, and nothing more was said. After a few minutes, Vargas grew bored and reached into a drawer where he had stashed a Playboy. Making sure to keep an eye on his partner, as well as the screen on his laptop, he quickly folded it into the cover of an equipment magazine before taking it out. As he leaned back into his chair, Jonesy looked up briefly and again reminded him to keep an eye on the screen.

True to his instruction, Vargas checked on the monitor two more times before all hell broke loose.

Jonesy sat at his desk, watching as his partner opened the door to the holding area, and wondered if maybe he should have gone instead. It was only the briefest of thoughts, and it was interrupted by the prisoner's voice, now chanting in a language he did not recognize.

"What the hell…"

For the second time in minutes, he jumped up from his chair. This time he walked around to his partner's desk and looked at the screen to see what was going on.

"Son of a bitch," he cried.

His partner was standing near the bars of the holding area, his tie firmly in Ronnie's hands and both seemed to be looking toward the stairs in fear. They stood in the world's brightest spotlight and he had only a moment to reflect upon this before he ran to the door at the top of the stairs.

"Vargas! Open the door," he yelled, pounding on the door next to the small window. From his point of view, he could just see the legs of his partner at the bottom of the stairs. He continued trying to get his partner's attention, calling his name and shouting various obscenities, but to no avail. Nothing was getting through to him. He could only continue to helplessly watch the events unfolding below.

"It is too late. He has come," the man in solitary said, breaking the momentary silence.

"What the fuck," Jonesy said incredulously.

At that moment, Vargas stepped backwards into the light at the bottom of the stairs. His face had become alarmingly white, his eyes filled with terror. Jonesy tried once again yelling at him to open the door, but there wasn't any response from his partner. As he watched, Vargas suddenly snapped his head back in the direction of the holding cell.

Jonesy began beating on the door again, yelling his partner's name repeatedly in an attempt to get his attention, but nothing seemed to be working. His partner's mouth slowly fell open as he began to slowly sway back and forth. He pressed his face against the glass of the window, trying to see what was going on down there when he heard a sound which would be the focal point of this memory for years to come.

From somewhere out of his line of sight, but directly in that of his partner's, there issued a low and visceral rattling unlike anything he had ever heard, which was then followed by a sickening crunch. A geyser of blood sprayed through the air, splashing onto his

25

partner and covering the ground, followed by two lesser spurts before finally stopping.

He continued to look on from above, frozen in horror, overcome with shock from the scene unfolding before him. There was no logical explanation to what he had just seen, and as he tried to get a grasp on it, Vargas turned his blank stare once more toward the small window. Droplets of blood were splattered across his face, dark in contrast to his ghostlike complexion, and his eyes were completely devoid of any humanity.

Jonesy futilely twisted and pulled at the doorknob. In the limited view from the window, he saw his partner's lips curl slightly upward at the sides. There was something chilling in the way he smiled. Something that didn't settle well with him at all, but before he could put a finger on it, the last bit of light vanished. Only the ghostly imprint that had been his partner's visage hovered in the darkness where he had moments ago stood.

He turned from the door, frantically looking around the office as he tried to think of what he should do. His gaze landed on his partner's desk, where he noticed the blackened monitor of the laptop staring back at him. He wasn't surprised that the screen was dark. There were no longer any lights to give him a clear picture of what was happening below. He continued to search the room, his eyes roaming from one desktop to the next, but it was the phone on his partner's desk that his eyes finally settled upon.

Finally broken from the grip of terror which had overcome him, he charged across the room and to the one thing that might just save him. Before he had stopped moving, his right hand was on the receiver of the phone, his left was frantically punching in the numbers, and he nearly would have slid past the desk altogether if his left foot hadn't caught on one of its legs. The line only rang twice before the person on the other end picked up.

"This is Haubbes."

"Captain! Oh thank God," he panted into the phone.

"Jonesy?"

"Captain, you've got to get someone over to the station right away, I need backup! The prisoner that came in tonight, I think he's escaped!"

"Whoa, slow down. Tell me exactly what happened."

Over the course of the next five minutes, Jonesy carefully reconstructed the details from the past twenty. Giving the same kind of detail he would to his work, he described everything that had happened, with the exception of the rattling he had heard just before he saw the blood.

"And you're sure that it's the prisoner?"

"Yes Ma'am."

"And Vargas is still down there?"

"Yes Ma'am."

"If what you are telling me is true, we have a very dangerous situation on our hands. Have you heard anything since the lights went out?"

"No ma'am, not a thing."

"And what about the prisoner? Any more unusual sounds coming from him?"

"Nothing ma'am."

"Okay, then I need you to listen to me very carefully, Officer Jones. Backup is on the way. Until it arrives, I don't want you to take your eyes off of the door. As of right now, we have to assume that the prisoner is armed and extremely dangerous. Don't do anything that will put yourself or the lives of anyone else in harm's way. You understand me?"

"Yes ma'am."

She disconnected from her end as he replaced the receiver back into its cradle. Moving slowly, he eased himself up into his seat and removed his sidearm from its holster. Without taking his eyes from the door, he flipped the safety off and leveled the gun at the center, just below its window. It was at that moment that the room thundered from a tremendous rumbling as the door was assaulted from the other side.

"Holy Mary, mother of God; pray for us now and at the hour of our death, amen."

The words stumbled over trembling lips, but they poured from his heart with strength that was tempered by decades of faith. As he continued his litany of prayer,

27

the door shuddered from the impact of another strong attack. Plaster dust fell from the ceiling, partially obscuring his view, but his aim remained steady. His focus was complete and as he continued to say what he believed to be his last words, a soft glow began to slip around the cracks of the drawer from which he had placed the prisoner's belongings.

Another blow finalized the destruction of the door, a door which was built to prevent this very thing from happening, and it exploded outward on its hinges. Standing in the darkness, just behind the frame of the door, was the slender form of a man around seven feet tall. Most of his features were completely hidden but for the two golden eyes that glared intensely from the shadows.

"Lord have Mercy," Jonesy uttered breathlessly. "Welcome to the A.S.P.D., motherfucker, the last place you'll see before I send you straight to Hell!"

IV

PUTTING THE PIECES TOGETHER

It hadn't been very long since the suspect had been taken to the station and dozens of emergency vehicles were still on the scene. In the short time since the first officer had arrived, the place had become a portrait of complete chaos. Not only were dozens of the A.S.P.D.'s best dutifully moving about, but she'd had to help call in several officers from the previous shift to contain the press and bystanders to the outside of the scene.

There were three helicopter's patrolling the skies above *The Clothing Store*, two were police manned while the third was from Channel 6 Action News. It was still dark, the sun was still a few hours away from rising, but one would be hard pressed to be fully aware of this while standing in the radius of the crime scene itself.

Several spotlights were set up around the perimeter, all of which had flooded the dock area near the back of the building. There were several bodies lying on the ground. They were perfectly laid side by side, thirteen in all. White sheets covered the bodies, each with its own distinctive red pattern staining it, and they were being attended to by a pair of busy coroners.

Those officers who had arrived first to the scene were standing nearest a small set of stairs leading up to the back room where most of the action had taken place, while others continued to walk in and out of the door at the top. Numbered markers were set up at various points of the scene, inside the building as well as out. The investigators were using them to piece together what had happened, while two other men walked around taking pictures as they processed the crime scene.

There are four vehicles inside of the parking lot; the coroner's car and three ambulances from All Saints Mercy. Six EMT's were slowly walking from body to body as well. They no longer have their bags with them and at this point are now only helping prepare their transport to the morgue.

At the entrance to the parking lot, and just to the right of the building, a reporter from Channel 6 and her crew are preparing to go live when the Captain arrives. They are forced to move aside as she drives her truck just into the entrance, where she then parks and shuts off the engine.

"Aw, come on Captain! You're blocking our shot," the reporter yelled from the sidewalk.

"Have a little respect for the dead. You'll get your shot as soon as they're out of here."

Having just stepped out of her truck when this exchange took place, Captain Nicoline Haubbes slams the door and looked around for the Lieutenant she'd left in charge of the scene.

The Captain looked fairly young for her age. Though she was just entering her fifties, she could easily pass for someone twenty years younger. Like Jonesy, she took care of herself religiously. For the last two decades, she had watched what she ate, preparing her meals from only the freshest foods. Her only exercise was a six mile jog every morning before work. Her body was a temple that she worked very hard to maintain, and it showed.

Her job also reflected her personal life in many ways. She was a perfectionist to the tenth degree. She expected her squad to do their jobs by following and enforcing the laws to their fullest extent. Nicoline had also been known to pull an officer to the side from time to time in order to instruct them on how to better do their jobs if she didn't like the way it was getting done.

She worked hard to keep her squad in the highest running order. She had been Captain for just a little over twenty years, one of the youngest women to ever fill her position in this line of work, and during her tenure, the number of violent crimes had gone down considerably. There were the still the odd cases that popped up every now and then, such as the murders over at the *Moving and Storage,* and now this, but for the most part, things were usually pretty quiet.

"Captain," her Lieutenant called to her. "Up here!"

He was standing on the dock, waving her over to the entrance leading into the back room. There were a couple of officers speaking to an E.M.T. near him, and as she approached he asked them to step aside so that they could talk.

"What the hell is going on here, Lieutenant?"

The Lieutenant, Jacob Combs, had been on the force only as long as she had been Captain. He was the epitome of the red-headed step child, complete with the freckles and glasses. What he lacked in appearance, however, he made up for in experience. Despite the fact that he perpetually looked like a rookie, he was one of the best cops that she had.

"Here's what we have; upon arriving at the scene, we found three different bodies. At least, we believe them to have once been bodies. Out front and along the side of the building," he points toward the street where her truck is parked, "were three piles of what can now only be described as, as 'goo', which we have very little chance of identifying. There was some clothing, as well as a few bits of jewelry mixed in with the substance and all of this has been bagged and tagged for later review."

"What about those," she asks while motioning the bodies beneath the sheets.

"Ma'am, those were most of what we found inside the building."

"Most? Explain."

"Yes ma'am. There are three different scenes in which these bodies were found. The first is right over there," he says while pointing toward the end of the dock.

"We found one body that appears to have fallen from the dock, while the other had crawled to the edge. Both died almost instantly from several gunshot wounds. Now, if you'll follow me…"

He turned and led her through the door leading into the loading area of the store. As they entered the room, now brightly lit by several lights like the ones outside, she noticed two separate areas where it looked as if gallons of blood had been dumped onto the floor. Directly to the left of where she stood was the first scene, which had the least amount of blood, while to the right it appeared as if a river of the coppery substance had recently spilled.

"We found seven of the bodies lying here," he motioned in front of him where the markers still lay. They seemed to be spread out in an almost perfect circle around another single marker.

"What's that one?"

"We found the body of a girl lying there. She had a large wound in her leg and a fatal wound in the chest. We also believe that she was with the perp."

The Captain nodded as she tried to imagine the battle that must have taken place.

"We also believe that she is responsible for the deaths of nine of those lying outside. We haven't confirmed it yet, but the positioning seems to be right. We'll know once the ballistics reports come back."

"What about over there?"

"This is where we believe the perp made his stand. Three of the most gruesome deaths took place there. He had cut the head and four fingers off of one and sliced open the abdomen of another. Yet another bled out from a gaping wound in the chest."

"What about number thirteen?"

"Huh?"

"There were thirteen of them outside. You've only mentioned twelve."

"Yes ma'am. He too died from a chest wound. Bled out right over there," he said while pointing to the side."

As she looked at the ground, she noticed another detail about the ground that was different from the first battle area.

"What's that," she asked while pointing to a powdery substance that was spread over the ground. She also noticed that there were bloody footprints leading from this area over to the first, prints which were also followed by a trail of ash. Those same prints lead from the first area to a door in the middle of the room, presumably to the front of the building, and then back out to the parking lot.

"We're not sure. We need to have some tests run, but it has the consistency of cremated remains."

She stood for a moment, as if lost in thought, while looking back from one battle scene to the other. The room looked as if a bomb had gone off at the very center, near the door leading to the front. Shelves, most of which had likely stood in the center of the room, were blown against the back wall of the building. There didn't seem to be any explosive damage beyond this, however. There was no blackened area or no residual fires to prove that it was indeed an explosion, only the warped and twisted remains of the shelving which had become a semi-permanent fixture to the wall.

"What in God's name caused THAT?!"

"We're not sure about that either, Captain. I've never seen anything like it."

"Is this it then?"

"No ma'am. It only gets worse from here on, I'm afraid."

"You're kidding, right?"

"I only wish I were… Please follow me."

Carefully threading his way around the markers and other investigators, he began to lead her to the door that led into the main store itself. She noticed that it was barely hanging on its hinges and appeared to have been broken at the lock.

"We had to take the ram to it," the Lieutenant explained as they approached.

"It had been barricaded from the inside."

"Wait, so the perp wasn't inside the actual building then?"

"No, he was only at the scene of the first battle. He had propped the girl up with her head in his lap and was unresponsive when we found him."

The Captain nodded as the Lieutenant pushed the broken door out of their way so that they could enter.

"Would someone please take care of this? Thank you!"

A couple officers hurried over to hold the ruined door open and then remove it once they were through.

The first thing she noticed was that it opened into a short hall about ten feet in length. The second was

33

that at the end of the hall was a large plastic tarp hanging from the frame.

"Captain? Before we go into the room just past that tarp, I have to warn you; it's bad. We have a small change station set up inside that little room off to the left there, where we'll need to put on some protective gear."

"What do you mean? We're not going to be in any danger, are we?"

"No ma'am, the gear is to protect the evidence and it will have to be collected once we leave," he answered solemnly.

They stepped into a small room initially set up for security. Several monitors showed images outside, one showed an image of the room they had just come from and a final showed nothing but static.

"Any footage of what happened?"

"No, it appears to have been a one-way setup and whoever was watching this is either outside or long gone."

On the other side of the room was a table with several vacuum sealed bags sitting on it. In each bag is a different article of clothing and there were several of each there for those who would need them.

Several minutes later, and with the help of her Lieutenant, each were covered from head to toe in white scrubs. They had white booties on their feet, gloves on their hands, a shower cap over their hair and a surgical mask over their mouths. The surgical masks had been scented from the inside to help prevent the wearer from smelling anything unpleasant.

"Must we really wear these," the Captain asked when he handed her one. He only nodded.

"What should I expect to see once we go past that tarp," she asked after putting on the mask. The smell was minty and not too unpleasant but she hated how it made her sound when she spoke.

"Words cannot describe it Captain. Only…"

She raised an eyebrow at his cryptic response, waving her hand impatiently for him to go on.

"Ma'am, forgive me. I don't want to talk about it. You'll have to see for yourself."

He walked past her and towards the tarp. As she
followed, beneath the minty aroma the mask was giving
her, she could detect something more sinister in the
air. It was a rotten, sour smell that attacked her
sensibilities, causing her to freeze in her tracks.
There was a small shop fan sitting on the floor a couple
of feet in front of the tarp. Several pine tree air
fresheners were fastened to the metal casing around it,
but the fan did little to keep the scent of death behind
the plastic covering. The Lieutenant looked over his
shoulder as he prepared to lift the tarp.

"What's on the other side of this tarp will change
your world forever," he spoke ominously. "I hope you
had a light dinner."

The tarp lifted and immediately she gagged from the
stench. It rolled out of the room in waves, reeking of
rotting flesh and bodily waste, and it effectively
choked her for several seconds before she was able to
calm her rolling stomach long enough to begin to look
around. Her eyes watered from the stench that hung in
the air, but what she saw in that room was something she
would have never imagined, nor would she ever forget.

She walked through the threshold, holding the tarp up
and away from her, into a room that was twenty foot long
by forty feet wide. There was trash bags piled against
the wall to her right, and in front of her, nearly
reaching to the ceiling, with the largest quantity of
bags being in the corner. Some of them were broken upon
at the bottom, from which slid the oozing remains of
what might have once been something that belonged to a
person. The first thing she finally managed to focus on
was a severed head that seemed to have rolled from the
nearest open bag. The flesh was melting from the skull,
and it was being aided along its state of decomposition
by dozens of plump maggots. She wretched involuntarily
as one burrowed into the head's right eye socket, its
back end wiggling in the air for a moment before it
vanished into the gelatinous orb.

Leaking from several other bags were similar sights,
but with different body parts. Out of one bag, she
could see several arms that had slid out of the opening
and onto the floor. Another seemed to be filled with

feet that were attached to various lengths of leg, while yet another contained hundreds of eyes, all of which seemed to stare at her with sightless accusation. Concentrated where the bags had been torn open, and flooding out towards the middle of the room, was a viscous liquid of pinkish color. Floating in the pink sludge were hundreds of dead flies, squirming maggots and bits of flesh that had come off the bodies of countless victims.

Her stomach contracted, causing another involuntary gag to force its way up her throat. She turned away from the horrific scent, trying to get control of herself, only to look upon the second most horrible thing in the room. In the front left corner of the room was a pile of bones. They filled the corner easily halfway to the ceiling and every one of them had been gnawed upon. There were still small chunks of tendon and flesh attached to each, and she made a long gagging noise when she was reminded of how a turkey leg looked after the meat had been picked from the bone.

On the wall to the left was another door that looked like it had been opened recently, the bones were pushed away from it in an outward swinging arc. Her eyes traveled further along the wall until they reached the corner of the room just to their left, to fall upon a pie shaped hole cut into the floor where the walls met. It was here that the smell of defecation was the strongest.

The Lieutenant motioned her back into the hall and to the little room with the cameras, where he sat her down. She didn't argue. When she had seen the bones, the color had drained from her face and she was instantly light headed. The makeshift toilet in the corner of the room had been the final straw. If he hadn't walked her out of there, she would have fainted.

"My God, Jacob," she finally managed. "What is going on here?"

He only shook his head miserably. When he next spoke, his voice was soft and it trembled uncharacteristically.

"There's more…"

She looked at him incredulously.

36

"What do you mean, there's more?"

"Downstairs… We found a room where they dismember the bodies. We also believe that they drain the blood of the victims beforehand, but for what purpose I cannot identify. There is…"

He chokes up, unable to continue for several more minutes.

"There's a child down there," he began.

"What? Is he alive?"

"I don't know what he is," he blurted.

"What do you mean y—," she started, but he was already up and leading her back to the room behind the tarp. He moved quickly, passing through the tarp and entering the room for the second time. They passed through it in a few short strides; neither saying a word nor sparing a second glance at the gruesome scene as they went straight into the door had been recently blocked by the bones. Behind the door was another room very similar to the one that they were just in, in width and length, only it did not contain the nightmare they had just passed through. This room, once the shop at the front of the building, was now set up as a large gambling room. There were three poker tables, complete with cards and chips, and all looking as if a game had been recently abandoned. There were also a couple blackjack tables, a craps table, and the far wall, behind which her truck was parked on the outside, had been made into a large bar.

"Where's th—," she was again cut off, but this time not by the Lieutenant. From somewhere to her left she heard a feral growling. She jumped, her hand flying down to her sidearm, but then she remembered that he had said the child was downstairs. On the wall to her left, and in its center, was the same door that twenty years ago an aging biker had died against. It was from behind that door that she was hearing the growls.

The Lieutenant placed his left hand over her right, the one on her sidearm, and shook his head.

"You're not going to need that. It's harmless as long as you don't get too close."

She noted that he had referred to the child as an 'it', but didn't question him any further, as she had

grown tired of his cryptic responses. As they were
weaving through the tables, from behind them a voice
called out to them;

"Lieutenant? Are you and Captain back there?"

It was the voice of their longtime coroner, David
Fitz, who was looking for them.

"Yeah. Just a second, okay," he called back.

"Sure, no problem. I just need you to sign off these
bodies so that we can move them."

"Alright. We're about to wrap this up back here,
we'll take care of it when we get back out."

They waited for moment, listening to David's
footsteps as he walked away, before going through the
door leading down the stairs.

"I gotta tell you Niki," he started. "Besides me,
you're going to be the only person to have seen what's
down these stairs. I- I couldn't bring myself to let
anyone else see it."

It was very rare when he called her by name, even
more so when he used it in nickname form. The last time
had been several years ago during a Christmas party and
he had been embarrassed for days because of it. There
wasn't going to be any of that here. He spoke as if to
a friend and his words came through tears at the thought
of what he was about to expose her to.

"Let's just get this over with, Jacob. Okay," she
asked while squeezing his shoulder.

"We'll take a look at this, child, and I'll decide
what we need to do from there. How does that sound?"

"Yes ma'am."

They opened the door and began walking onto the
stairs. They were made of iron and the design was very
much like that of a fire escape. The stairs were
suspended by a weighted pulley system, over the floor
below, and as they stepped onto them, they began to
lower to the floor.

"Why the raised stairs," she asked more to herself.

"My guess is for what they didn't want let out."

"*What…*" she asked quizzically, placing emphasis on
the word he had just used.

"Exactly," was all he could offer in response.

The stairs thudded on the concrete below, at the bottom of which was a large oak door. It was an arched, plank style door with iron bars over a small window near the top. It had a French door styled handle, and as Jacob reached for it, she began to feel a creeping sense of dread at what she was about to see.

The door slowly creaked inward, revealing a large room, at the end of which she saw a huge kettle-shaped boiler. The base was round with a grated door large enough to fit a casket through. Ducts snaked away from it in all directions and into various points in the ceiling, giving it the appearance of the world's largest steam-punk octopus.

On the wall to their left were two doors, the nearest of which would lead directly below the horrific room they had passed through to get here. The second was farther back and presumably led to a room that would be somewhere below where the bodies had been discovered.

"Is that…" she started to ask as she pointed to the door on the right.

"Yeah," he answered softly. "That's where it is."

"What's behind those other doors?"

He only shook his head as he led her to the room from which the snarling continued. It was low, like the warning from a dog when you get too close to its food bowl, or its master's property, and very much inhuman.

"Jesus, are you sure that's a child in there?"

"No," he answered after taking a deep breath, "I'm not sure of anything anymore."

He reached out and grabbed the doorknob, turning it for what felt like an eternity. She watched, fascinated, as he turned the knob all the way around before pulling the door toward them. As the door cracked upon, the smell of rotting meat wafted out and blasted through the flimsy barrier covering her face.

"Oh my GOD," she sputtered.

From inside the room came a burst of activity. The sound of chains rattling, followed by the most primal howl she had ever heard, causing her to jump and as she began to move backward Jacob reached over and grabbed her right arm, holding her in place. He must have seen the panic that she was feeling because he only shook his head and began to pull her toward the room, a room inside which she no longer wanted to see the '*what*' he had cryptically spoken of earlier.

Her every instinct screamed to her that what was on the other side of this door was something she wasn't meant to see, while her mind cried betrayal when he continued to pull her toward it. The door finally swung open before her, revealing a small room that appeared to be more like a makeshift prison. The walls were stone and mortar, and it was the one opposite the door to which the child was chained. Suspended from the wall were two large rings, through which were the very thick gauged chains that held the child-like creature.

The mechanism was simple. On one end of the chains were a large weight the total of which was approximate to the weight of the person on the other end, and this is what the Captain and the Lieutenant were now looking at.

The child's hands were suspended above its head, manacled by the writs, to the chains. He had strikingly dark auburn hair, short and at one time well kempt. Now it sat matted against his skull, glued down by a substance that was difficult to see with just the light that came in through the door. His eyes were completely white. There were no pupils, but this didn't detract the feeling that he was looking straight at them. His face was caked in dirt, grime and something that looked a little like blood.

The child was naked, except for a dirty pair of underwear. Cuts and scrapes covered the majority his body, but most horrifying was the flap of skin that hung over his exposed kneecap. She tried to look away several times, but the fact that no blood seemed to be pouring from it kept drawing her back. His belly was distended, impossibly full for his small frame, and it quivered with each hate filled snarl.

His feet were and hands were torn to shreds. The flesh was torn away and cracked, with each gaping wound caked in the same nasty substances that were smeared on his face.

The creature, because nobody in their right mind could call this thing a child, lunged forward, reaching towards them with manic fervor. Its teeth clacked together, snapping with the ferocity of a wild dog. It reached its limit, however, just inches before the Captain's face, its fetid breath blowing upon her its deadly promise.

She stood hypnotized from the shock of seeing what was before her, rooted firmly in place, and if it hadn't been for her Lieutenant yanking her out and slamming the door; the creature would have taken a good amount of her face with it.

"Jesus! What the fuck IS that thing Jacob!?"

He was trembling, leaning against the wall with his arms wrapped tightly around himself. His face had grown pale, and with his complexion he was nearly as white as the sheets they had used to cover the bodies outside.

"I don't know, Niki. I've never seen anything like it in my life."

"Did you SEE that?! It just tried to eat my fucking face off!"

He could barely respond. His eyes had glazed over and he stared blankly at the door.

"Jacob," she shouted a little louder than she had intended.

He blinked, eyes light green eyes filling with tears.

"Let's get out of here, okay?"

His nodded as she placed a hand on his back. This time it was her guiding him away from the horror.

"This stays between us," she said soothingly. "There's no reason that we need to tell anyone else about what's in there."

They reached the stairs and she pulled them back down to the floor. As they were climbing them to the top, her cell phone began to ring.

"This is Haubbes."

"Captain? Oh thank God," Jonesy panted into the phone.

Several minutes later she put the phone back in her pocket. During the conversation, they had made their way through an army of investigators, back to the outside of the building, and were now signing the papers for the coroner.

"What's the rush David? You know I could have filled these out in the morning, right?"

He looked up to her with an apologetic look on his face, fearfully glancing at the Lieutenant before answering.

"I know Captain, and I'm sorry about that, but I didn't want to take any chances with this one. I would feel better if this part of this nasty business were out of the way."

She smiled kindly at him, patting him on the shoulder before she walked past.

"Let me know when you have your preliminary reports done, okay?"

"Of course."

As she and the Lieutenant neared her truck, she turned to him and gave him a stern look.

"You probably got a good idea of what's going on from my side of the conversation, so I'm wont to say that I need you to stay here. Seal off the basement, for now, and if anyone has a problem with that, you make sure to direct them to me. Round up some of your men and send them my way. Make sure that when they leave, they do so with no sirens and that they take different routes back to the station. There's no need for us to give the press any reason to tag along."

"Yes ma'am," he paused for a moment, as if he were seeking the courage to ask something.

"Out with it already. There isn't any more time for chatter."

"It's nothing. I'll talk with you later, after we've cleaned this up. Be careful, okay?"

She smiled at him before climbing behind the wheel. In the distance the sky was beginning to lighten, signaling the approaching dawn. She shook her head when she realized just how long she had been here and put her truck into drive, glancing only briefly in the rearview mirror as she left the scene.

Jacob remained where she had left him for several minutes, watching as she drove her truck up and through the crowds at the entrance, before turning around to follow her orders. It had been a long night, but he knew that the day was going to be even longer. There

were many pieces in this puzzle, and it was going to be
a champion's task putting it all back together.

V

THE AFTERMATH

"Officer Jones?"

A dark blanket lay over his consciousness, dampening his senses and leaving behind an apathetic shell of the man he once was.

"Jonesy? Where are you?!"

He vaguely felt something warm in his left hand. It seemed to radiate a soothing heat that was subtle, yet comforting, and it wasn't altogether unfamiliar to him. The sensation was only a passing interest, however, and it faded quickly into the back of his thoughts. For the moment, he was content to merely stare into the dark shroud around him and enjoy the warm feeling pulsing from his hand.

"He's over here," shouted a voice that sounded eerily familiar. He felt like he should know who it belonged to but the name danced merrily at the edges of his memory. A set of hands grabbed him on either shoulder, gently shaking him while the familiar voice grew more urgent.

"Lachlan, damnit, wake up!"

Whoever was trying to rouse him lifted their hand from his right shoulder and seconds later cracked it across his right cheek.

White lightning pierced his comforting darkness, shooting from every direction as it chased away the dark veil, and forced him to return to consciousness. When he finally opened his eyes, his fears presented to him the last image he had seen standing in the doorway. It was a man whom everyone knew of, and who is emulated no less than once per year. He had been in the nightmares of millions for centuries.

Officer Lachlan Jones, better known as "Jonesy" to his friends, looked upon the face of Dracula and screamed. Terror boiled up from the very depths of his soul, a soul which shook in fear knowing that it could be denied its place in Heaven, and took control of every fiber in his body. He shrieked until the breath was gone from his lungs, his face frozen in silent rictus at

*that which stood before him. And when the air in his
lungs was no more, he drew in a deep breath and shrieked
until his throat grew scratchy and his voice, hoarse.*

*Stepping out from the shadows was a man of
extraordinary height, who, not counting his hair, was an
intimidating seven feet high. He had to stoop as he
crossed the threshold, as well as turn slightly to the
side, to allow the passage of his broad shoulders. His
hair was raven black, slicked stylishly back and to the
side. He wore a black tuxedo with a white ruffled shirt
and red cummerbund. Around his neck was a golden
pendant which depicted a shining sun with a dragon at
its center. Six stars surrounded the edge of the sun
and as he watched, the dragon seemed to slowly turn its
mighty bejeweled gaze upon him.*

*The man was a rugged kind of handsome, with smooth
pale skin and bright red lips. Though they had earlier
been the color of amber, his eyes were now dark and
menacing. As he stepped into the light, a thin membrane
peeled away from them, revealing eyes that were true to
his form. Much like a reptile, he had opened his eyes
from the left and right. As if to affirm this, they
blinked quickly before vanishing once more. He looked
upon Jonesy with his beguiling eyes, eyes which were a
rich shade of crimson and brimming over with evil
intent.*

*He felt a dark veil falling over his vision and as he
looked into the eyes of the monster he felt his mind
slipping away from his control.*

Another flash of lightning and the Count was gone.
His right cheek stung as if pierced by the stingers of a
thousand bees and his head reeled from the blow. His
vision was blurry, and the memory of the last few
moments was beginning to fade as he came to. He looked
fearfully to the remnants of the holding cell door, but
he couldn't see past the small crowd gathered there.

He tried to hear what was going on around him, but
his sense of hearing had yet to fully recover from the
dazed state that he had been awakened from. There was a
pressure on his left shoulder as someone gently squeezed
it, and he could just make out someone speaking to him.

"…nesy? Can you hear me buddy?"

He blinked as the fog covering his senses finally lifted. The officer in front of him was Richie Cooklan, a rookie who usually worked the dayshift. But that couldn't be, could it? It would be another couple of hours before he came on duty!

The room was bustling with activity and his ears were assaulted by the sounds of phones ringing, and a cacophony of voices talking at once. From his vantage, he could see that he had been moved to a cot in one of the side offices.

"Wha—," he began, pausing long enough to change his line of questioning.

"How long have I been out," he asked instead.

"Jonesy, thank God!"

"Easy kid," he said as he tried to sit up. He winced as he felt a sharp pain in the palm of his left hand. He lifted it to see that it was wrapped heavily in bandages.

"Yeah, it was the damndest thing! When we came in, you were holding the weirdest cross I had ever seen. You were holding it so tightly that blood was pouring from your hand!"

He frowned, not remembering having done that, and repeated his last question.

"Oh, it's been four hours since you called the Captain, and it's been crazy here. I mean, with what they found at The Clothing Store, and now with Ronnie being dead, and Vargas missing-"

"Wait, what do you mean 'Vargas is missing'?"

"It's like I said. He's just, gone Sir! And then, well, there's you-"

"What about me, kid?"

"Well sir," he looked away, embarrassed, and there was a brief pause before he continued.

"Sir, you were screaming; 'The Dragon has Come', over and over. You were seriously freaking some of us the fuck out. Sir."

Jonesy jerked as the image of the medallion swam into memory.

"The prisoner! The one they brought in from The Clothing Store, where is he?"

46

A funny look came over Cooklan's face, who glanced furtively toward the small crowd outside the office. Jonesy followed his gaze, his own landing on the small group of people milling about in the office.

At that moment the Captain, the coroner, and two others emerged from the wrecked doorframe leading down. Her face was pale, and she looked more tired than he ever recalled having seen her, but she continued to give out orders to his squad-mates.

"I think you need to speak to the Captain about that," he finally answered.

At that exact moment, she looked over and their eyes met. She finished speaking with the coroner, and after giving the other officers their orders, she made her way to the office.

"Cooklan, I need you to assist outside," she said upon entering.

"Yes ma'am."

After he exited, she closed the blinds and locked the door. She didn't immediately turn around, however, and as she stood there her shoulders slumped.

"I don't know what's going on anymore Lachlan," she finally admitted after several moments.

He moved up behind her and placed his hands on the outside of her arms. She turned and buried her face into his chest as every emotion that had risen up within her over the last few hours rushed out in a flood.

Several minutes pass as the two continue to embrace one another, each drawing upon the other for support during a situation that neither has the experience to handle. They hold onto one another while the world outside continues to pick up the pieces, afraid to let go until they are able to regain their composure.

Finally, she takes a step back, places her hands upon his chest and looks up into his eyes with a measure of gratitude. He nods and smiles in return, but his eyes are still filled with worry.

"The prisoner? Did we get him?"

The events of the last few hours had become jumbled together and his questions only confused her. Her first thought was of Ronnie, whom they had found the remains

47

of inside the holding cell, and what he was asking didn't make any sense to her.

This passed, as it dawned on her that he had been speaking of the other.

"He didn't tell you, did he," she asked breathlessly.

"Tell me what?"

"That man that we brought in from *The Clothing Store*? He was still in his cell when we got here."

Jonesy's mouth fell open in disbelief.

"Wha-t? That's impossible," he stammered.

"So is the fact that a door meant to keep in the toughest of prisoners was battered down from the inside" she barked. "Or how about how one of our regulars was decapitated and completely drained of blood from behind locked doors? Tell me, Lachlan, where the fuck is his head? And we still don't know where the hell Vargas is!"

At that moment there came a knock at the door.

"Captain? We've got him ready in the interrogation room whenever you're ready."

"Thank you, we'll be there in a minute," she answered.

It was Jonesy's turn to be puzzled. Sensing the question that was coming, she beat him to the punch.

"After removing the body, I had the prisoner brought up to the interrogation room. Jacob will be releasing a statement soon about what happened at the crime scene so you'll be with me on this."

She paused, regarding him before asking the next question.

"Are you okay to do this?"

He only nodded in response and walked over to the cot on which he had awakened. Reaching down, he grabs his gunbelt and fastens it around his waist.

"How's your hand," she asked softly when she noticed him wincing.

"It's really sore," he answered sheepishly. "But there's something I don't understand. Cooklan said that I had been holding the cross that belongs to the prisoner."

"How is that possible? Didn't you file it away in the evidence room?"

48

He shook his head in denial before continuing.

"No, I wasn't going to be able to get to it until after I had finished filing the reports. The last thing I remember was-" He trailed off as he struggled to remember just exactly what it was that had happened. He had just disconnected with the Captain when-

"What," she asked when he only shook his head in confusion.

"I can't remember. I sure as hell don't remember unlocking or opening the drawer I had placed his things in. Not that I could have unlocked it if I had wanted to!"

"What do you mean?"

"Vargas had the goddamn keys!"

There was no way either of them could explain how the drawer was opened. She had the only other key to the drawer and his had been on the key-ring that was found on the floor outside of the main holding cell.

"We'll talk about that later," she finally admitted. "Right now I need to get some answers."

She turned and opened the door to the main office. As it was when she had closed the door, the change in her stature was immediate. No longer did she appear the vulnerable woman who had turned to Jonesy for comfort. As soon as she walked through the threshold and into the chaos outside, she took on the air of authority that she had worn so well over the years.

"Captain! What should we do with any incoming 'guests'?"

"Take them down and put them in solitary until the repairs are made."

"Captain? We have a call on hold with-"

"Deal with it," she answered, briskly cutting the speaker off.

They passed through the main office and through another door which opened into a small hallway. There were three rooms off of this hall, two on their left and one off of their right, with a final door at the end of the hall leading to the evidence room. Jonesy felt a twinge of regret upon looking at this final door, as he knew he should have gone there before working on any of the reports.

"Jonesy?"

"Sorry Captain," he stammered, "I was just thinking of something."

"Are you sure you want to do this," she asked, searching his eyes with her own.

"Yes, sorry. I think I need to get some answers as well, and I have a feeling that, whatever the outcome, we'll find them behind that door." He nodded toward the first door on the left, which was the first of two interrogation rooms, and resumed walking toward it. As he walked past her, she placed a hand on his right arm.

"What happened back there Lachlan?"

"I don't know," he sighed as he rubbed his eyes with his good hand, "but I pray to God that he can give me an answer that will make some sense."

She cocked an eyebrow in confusion, wondering just how their prisoner would have any answers, but the moment between them had passed. As he lowered his hand away from his eyes, he redirected it to the doorknob and turned it, pushing the door open to the room beyond. She let her hand fall away from his arm and followed him in, closing the door behind them once they were both inside.

The prisoner sat behind the only table in the room with his head buried in his hands. His long, dark auburn hair hung about his head and completely obscured his face from view. It was still matted in some places from the blood that was in it, though they had yet to determine who the blood belonged to, if ever that were possible. His duster had been removed, as well as the weapon's harness for the crossbow and the holster for the pistol he carried, but beyond that he still wore the clothes he had been brought in with.

He wore a light blue shirt, button up and long sleeved, which was tucked into his blue jeans, and light brown leather boots over his feet. There was a considerable amount of blood on his shirt, presumably from the female victim they had found, the most prominent detail being the handprint near his left shoulder. They both also knew that he also had a bloody handprint on his face, but it was impossible to see behind his hair.

Standing against the far wall, and to either side of the prisoner, are two officers whose sole duty was to guard him.

"That will be all gentlemen," she directed their way, "we'll take it from here."

When they were alone with the prisoner, she sat at the chair across from him while Jonesy stood just off to her right. There was a small folder sitting in front of her, inside of which were photographs from the crime scene. There was also a pen and a small notebook on the table for her to keep track of any information he might give during the investigation. Normally they would conduct an interrogation only after first pulling the suspect's records, but tonight has been all but normal.

"I am Captain Haubbes, and this," she said while motioning her thumb over her shoulder, "is Officer Jones. Now, would you mind telling us your name?"

She opened up the small notebook and looked across the table at him expectantly. There hadn't been any change since they entered, and for all they knew he could have been asleep. She waited only for a moment for an answer before she spoke again.

"We're in an uncomfortable position with this case. So far as we can figure, we have the person responsible for at least fourteen deaths, seventeen if you count the three piles of gore we found," she paused briefly for effect, "on the outside."

The man stirred at this, lifting his head enough to look at her from behind his soiled hair.

"I'll be brutally honest with you here. We know that you aren't responsible for nine of the victims and we're sure that ballistics will prove that, but because the female isn't in any shape to talk about it, the charges are likely to pass onto you unless you cooperate with us."

She paused, distracted by his grayish colored eyes. The grey was dark, lifeless and accentuated by golden flecks that were spread out around the pupil. As she spoke, he watched her with feigned interest, his eyes cold and calculating. She could see an unsettling intelligence in those eyes, one that had likely been developed over years of experience.

51

"Ecce non est auxilium mihi in me et necessarii quoque mei recesserunt a me," he finally spoke, much to their confusion.

Jonesy jerked as he vaguely remembered hearing the same kind of low chant from before. It had been hard to hear the first time, but it had been there beneath the frantic cries of Ronnie and his partner.

"What the hell IS that," he asked in exasperation.

"I'm sorry, we don't understand," the Captain followed.

"Do you know any English?"

The prisoner only continued to silently watch her, offering no sign of understanding to her questioning.

"Jonesy, is there anything familiar about his dialect to you?"

He thought about it for a moment before answering.

"There is, now that you mention it" he trailed off in thought for a brief moment before continuing.

"Captain, a word?"

He motioned to the door and stepped out into the hallway. When she joined him shortly after, she had a mild look of irritation in her expression.

"What is it that you couldn't say in there?"

"There are a couple of things, actually. One, I'm sure I heard him speaking in that language earlier, when he was still in lockup."

"Okay, and the other?"

"There IS something familiar about the language, but I'm going to need some time."

"Time isn't something that we have, Lachlan. You know damn well that if we don't get this under control, the State will take it out from under us."

"Just give me a couple of hours, Niki. I promise, if this pans out, we'll be able to get the upper hand on this."

"You better be right. If we lose this one, it might mean both of our jobs."

"Trust me. I have an old favor to call in, and I believe this is what I've been saving it for."

She nodded her reluctant approval, afraid to say anymore, and she watched as he rushed down the hall and through the door to the office.

"This had better work," she said more to herself than to anyone else.

After sending the two officers back in to watch over him, she also left the hall and re-entered the main office. She noticed that the contractors who were hired to replace the door had finally arrived and were hard at work. Her crime scene investigators were slowly trickling out, having done as much as they could, and the evidence was now being processed.

"*Jonesy's going to have his hands full tonight*," she thought as she watched last of the evidence being moved to the back.

Knowing that she was going to be just as busy, she made her way through the main office and towards her own, giving orders as she went. She knew that things were going to have to get back to normal quickly, and in order for that to happen, everyone had to be on top of their game. She wanted nothing more than for her precinct to be running like a well-oiled machine, and with any luck, she would be able to retain some form of command when the State Patrol did finally arrive.

"Cooklan!"

"Yes ma'am," the rookie yelled from across the room. He had been helping carry the battered door away from the frame when she called to him and he now stood as frozen as a deer caught in the headlights. She motioned for him to follow her as walked into her office.

"Go ahead," an available construction worker said, taking his place.

"Thanks buddy."

A moment later, he stood across from his Captain, who was now seated at her desk.

"You called for me?"

"Yes. I need you to find out when the Lieutenant will be giving his press release."

"I believe that should be happening right now, ma'am."

As he answered her, she reached down to open the slender drawer in front of her and removed a small remote. By the time the rookie had finished speaking she had pointed it to a flat screen TV on the wall to her right and had hit the power button.

"Sir! Over here, Sir!"

The Lieutenant stood behind a small podium that had been set up across the street from the crime scene. It was placed in such a way that the building could be seen over his shoulder. Several people were gathered in front of him, each vying over the other for his attention.

"Please, one at a time," he spoke with raised hands.

While there were only a couple reporters on the scene, Haubbes recognized several of the others as being journalists for physical and online news mediums from surrounding areas.

"Lieutenant," the reporter from Channel 6 News called out. "Can you tell us a little about what happened here last night?"

The small gathering murmured loudly in agreement to the question while a couple of voices called questions of their own. Raising his hand to signal their silence, he nervously licked his lips before he began to speak.

"Details at this time are still a little sketchy and until we know the full extent of what happened here, we will not be releasing any names at this time. From what we do know; two people arrived at the building behind me early this morning and killed several employees who were working inside."

"Lieutenant!?" The voice belonged to a slender man near the middle of the group. She recognized him as a journalist for the Golden Sun, a local and one of the few remaining newspapers.

"Yes," he answered, signaling for him to continue.

"There were reports of several gunshots. Can you tell us approximately how many people died, and, if there were any survivors?"

"At this time, we're not able to release that information until we more about what happened here."

The crowd grumbled unhappily while another voice toward the back called for his attention.

"Sir," a redheaded woman with freckles on her face called out. Niki recognized her as a well known online journalist and blogger known for her extremist opinions.

"I was one of the first here, aside from Channel 6, and couldn't help but notice someone being loaded into

54

the back of an ambulance. I'm no doctor, but I could tell by the way the E.M.T.'s were hustling, that this person was a survivor. Do you care to comment on that?"

The crowd fired off several questions at the same time and Niki cursed as the situation began to deteriorate.

"Damn it Jacob, you were supposed to be giving a press release, not a Q and A," she growled at the TV.

"Please" Jacob yelled on the TV. "At this time we cannot give any details until we know the full extent of what has happened here."

When it began to look like things were going to go completely out of control, Jacob spoke one last time before walking off of the camera.

"At this time we CAN tell you that we do have a suspect in custody. There is very little reason at this time for us to believe that there was anyone else involved. We will continue to investigate the crime scene, and we will release more information as we have it. Thank you, that is all for now."

Niki clicked the power off with her remote and tossed it to her desk with a clatter, lowering her face into her hands and groaning in exasperation.

"Ahem?"

She had forgotten about the rookie and jumped at the sound of his voice.

"Your orders, ma'am" he asked nervously. It was obvious that he was uncomfortable about still being here and that he didn't know what to do from this point.

"Sorry," she started shakily. "Go assist with our internal problem as much as you possibly can. I also want you to get with David on this and let me know when he has something."

"Yes ma'am!"

"Oh, and when Jonesy returns, please send him into my office."

The rookie nodded, thankful to have a reason to get out of here, and closed the door behind him as he left. She sat there for several minutes, staring at the back of the door, trying to think of the last time she had felt like she was in control.

"It's been too long," she surmised, *"and it is going to be even longer before this fiasco is over."*

For the second time in several minutes, she lowered her face into her hands and watched helplessly as the horrors from this morning began to replay before her

.

She walked past the bodies lined up in the parking area on the side of the building, only now the sheets were drawn back from pallid faces that stared at her accusingly. While none of them appeared to be innocent, with their facial modifications and evil looking tattoos, all watched her with an equal amount of rancor.

She entered the room beyond the tarp and several eyeballs rolled across the floor to create a single lined path to the second door she had passed through, left of the one she had just entered. They were two rows deep on either side of her and each turned to follow her progress as she passed.

She was in the basement, standing before the creature chained to the wall and knee-deep in the half eaten remains of its countless victims. Only this time, the creature didn't seem to mind her presence. It was holding onto a leg that had been broken off below the knee and was ripping the flesh away with its teeth. The childlike creature looked up at her and she saw not the face of a child but that of the suspect still sitting in the interrogation room. It held the leg out to her, as if it were an offering, and began to speak. Black inchor began to ooze from the corners of its mouth and it spoke words which came from the darkest depths of its evil soul.

"Et comedes fructum uteri tui et carnes filiorum et filiarum tuarum quas dedit tibi Dominus Deus tuus in angustia et vastitate qua opprimet te hostis tuus"

The words rolled over her like cold water, startling her, and she was jerked back to reality by the sound of her involuntary cry.

COMING TO

…the patient's eyes slowly opened, blinking several times as they adjusted to the light that was shining into them. From somewhere nearby is a steady electronic beeping, followed by the occasional buzzing of a printer as it dutifully made records of the patient's progress.

The walls of the room are creamy white and there is little decoration on them, with the exception of a simple cross on the wall to the right of the bed. Against the wall to the left is a small couch, with room enough for maybe two people, over which is a window that has the shades pulled tight.

There is the pungent odor of cleaner in the air, most prominent but for the scent of fresh flowers that can be detected just beneath it. The patient turned a little more to the right and notices an open door leading into a smaller room, presumably a bathroom, and sitting on a small table in the corner is a vase filled with roses.

At the foot of the patient's bed, a door quietly opens and the room is suddenly filled with the chatter of several people busily going about their work on the other side. Following the approach of a single pair of footsteps, the door silently closes and the only remaining sound is the padding of their feet as they approach the bedside.

"I see you're awake, Mrs. Doe. We have much to talk about, you and I. How about we start with your name?"

The patient turned her head up toward the sound of the voice, but her vision had yet to clear. The form of the speaker is blurry and she tries several times to blink it into focus but to no avail. Her lips, cracked, slowly part as she desperately tries to speak her first words in several days.

"…irsty…"

"Yes, of course you are, how silly of me," the voice muttered almost to itself. The form bent forward and placed one hand gently behind her head, lifting her towards the small plastic cup the other was bringing to her lips. Seconds later, the cold, refreshing rush of water flooded into her mouth, revitalizing the dry skin over her lips and refreshing her body as she drank greedily.

She winced as she felt a sharp pain in her chest, eliciting a small gasp from the person assisting her, and a small groan escaped her as she was laid back against her pillow.

"I'm so sorry, I hadn't thought about your injuries. I hope I haven't hurt you too much?"

"N-no," she stammered.

The water was taking its affect as she already felt a little stronger than she had before drinking it.

"Good! Now, if you think you're up to it, would you mind telling me your name? There are a few gentlemen who will want to speak to you soon, but only if I think you're up to it, of course."

She opened her mouth to respond but little more than a squeak came out. A small look of consternation crossed over her features, as she tried to recall that which she should have easily known, and she struggled internally with the question for several moments before the person aiding her finally spoke up.

"It's okay, it will come to you soon enough. No need to force it. What you need now is some rest. *They* will have to wait until tomorrow I'm afraid."

She squinted in a final effort to see who she was speaking to, but her vision simply wouldn't clear enough for her to make out the person now reading something just to the left of her head.

"How did I get here," she managed to finally ask. She didn't know why it was important to her, but something inside needed to know the answer.

"A young Sergeant brought you, though his name slips me for some reason. Then again, I wasn't on duty when you came in. He must have been a looker though. Natalie, she was on duty that night, was pretty taken with him."

She was disappointed when she didn't hear the answer she was looking for, but it didn't last for very long. As the nurse continued to speak, she drifted quietly back into unconsciousness…

VI

A WORLD YOU'VE NEVER IMAGINED

His heart was heavy, broken, and beating to an increasingly familiar tune of despair. Never in his long life had he felt as far away from himself as he did at that very moment, and he looked through what he felt were stranger's eyes. Everything had taken on a dreamlike quality after discovering his best friend and sometimes lover lying in a growing pool of her own blood. Deep in his heart, where he had once grasped onto the final thread of his faith, was now an empty void, barren of even the smallest ray of hope.

His hands were clasped before him, cuffed and attached to a chain that led to his manacled feet, and were resting just inches away from a series of pictures spread out on the table. Each image depicted the more than a dozen bodies found in the large room where he had been arrested, but the one he kept returning to was that of the person who had trusted him the most over the last few days.

His chest hitched as a strangled sob worked its way out of his deepest depths, coming forth as a moan so full of grief that the two officers behind him shifted uncomfortably at their posts.

He tried to look away from the picture, searching for anything else that might help take his mind away from the painful memory, but there was no escaping it, or her. His hands were still stained with the blood that had poured from her wounds, and he could feel it crusted upon his cheek each time his face took on a different expression.

From behind him, the two officers looked at each other and silently agreed on their next action. Stepping forward, they quickly shuffled the pictures together and in an act of compassion very unusual for this type of situation, they turned them over and placed them back into the folder left behind by their Captain.

"...thank you," he whispered gratefully. The officer to his right placed a hand on his shoulder and gently squeezed before they stepped back to their posts behind him. The gesture had been simple enough, but the meaning behind it was enough to soothe his aching heart, giving him a brief repose from the burden it carried.

Their act of kindness allowed him to finally see through the veil of grief, which had blinded him since the battle, and he looked around for the first time since being brought into this room. Across from the table, he saw the only door in or out of the room. It was a simple wooden door with only two panels, a larger rectangular one over a smaller square panel, and the only thing that made it unusual was that it was made from Walnut.

The door sat between two reflective sheets of glass which filled nearly the half of the wall. While they only looked like mirrors from the inside, from the outside, as many as six people could comfortably watch the events unfolding inside the interrogation room. The room was lit by small light-bulbs from the inside of several cuplike openings, and they effectively chased away every shadow, revealing the room in its drab entirety.

In contrast to the dark Walnut of the door, the walls were smooth and concrete gray and aside from a set of speakers above the door, there were no other adornments that he could see. Leaning back enough so that he could see past his knees, he finally noticed that the table and his chair were bolted to the floor.

From behind him one of the officers cleared his throat, possibly the one who had shown him an ounce of comfort not too long ago, politely reminding him to sit up in his chair. No sooner did he comply when the door opened and the man earlier identified as Officer Jones stepped inside. This time, he was alone as he walked into the room and took a seat across from him.

Jonesy reached across the table and grabbed the small folder, frowning for a moment when he realized something was out of place, and pulled it in front of him. As he had not yet been to the crime scene, he spent several moments going through the photographs inside before setting it back down on the table.

John watched patiently as this took place, his face blank and unreadable to the other. Officer Jones placed his elbows on the table on either side of the folder and

rested his chin thoughtfully on his fists, studying him
for a moment before leaning back and speaking.

"Who was she," he finally asked.

"My best friend," John answered softly. His voice
was raspy, conducted by abused vocal chords, and he
coughed gently to clear it.

"Why don't you tell me a little about her?"

"We first met when she was a little girl. Her family
had been traveling cross country when they'd had-" He
paused for a moment as he contemplated how to safely
finish his thought. "-an accident. She had been the
only survivor, whom I had rescued moments before their
vehicle exploded. I have been in her life ever since."

"Who was she," Jonesy repeated impatiently. "Her
name?"

"Chloe Hudson," he answered shortly.

Officer Jones rubbed his chin with his right hand as
he pondered the name.

"And is that her legal name," he finally asked.

"Yes," John replied. This time it was his turn to
show impatience through his actions, but it was
completely overlooked by the policeman.

"Seems like I should know that name," he said softly
to himself.

A few minutes passed as Jonesy studied the man across
from him. He thought about the answers he had been
given and about how the man's eyes hadn't shown any
deception as he spoke them.

"Do you want to tell me YOUR name," he finally asked.

"Shouldn't you be writing all of this down," John
countered.

"Don't you worry about that, Sir, it's all being
taken care of. Now, please tell me your name."

"John Rizzerio."

"Rizzerio. Isn't that a holy name?"

"I believe you're thinking of the saint Rizzerio, who
was born in the twelfth century and who was also the
adviser and closest friend to Francis…"

"Possibly," he acceded carefully, "but we both know
that you are no Saint, don't we Mr. Rizzerio?"

John's expression didn't change as he returned the
man's stare, and when it became obvious to the other

61

that he wasn't going to take the bait, Jonesy continued
with his line of questioning.

"You're in quite a bit of trouble, you know that
don't you? Do you want to tell me about the events that
led up to this," he said while spreading pictures of The
Clothing Store's interior before him. When John didn't
answer his question, he leaned forward and pushed the
picture of Chloe over to him.

"By our accounts, she did most of the work. Based on
the weapons that she had on her and the bodies around
her when we arrived, I'd say she took down nine to your
four, am I correct? What if I was to tell you that
because of her, condition, we could pin all of them on
you?"

"Qui autem me audierit absque terrore requiescat et
abundantia perfruetur malorum timore sublato."

Jonesy looked over his shoulder just to the right of
the door before turning back to John with his next
question.

"What is that you're speaking there? Mind sharing?"

"There is much I could tell you, but, I am concerned
that you wouldn't find much sleep afterwards. The
nightmares would haunt you."

"Mister, I have seen things today that no person
should ever have to. Nightmares are the least of my
worries at the moment. What I am worried about now are
answers and you can start by telling me about what
happened."

"To what end?"

"Excuse me?"

"To what end, Officer Jones? It seems to me that you
already have your minds made up based on the images
you've spread out before me. I think you're afraid
because you don't know why any of this has happened and
you're looking for a quick way to get out of having to
deal with it."

Jonesy leapt to his feet, his chair flying out from
behind him, and slammed his fists on the table before
him.

"I don't give a FUCK what you think, Mr. Rizzerio!
What I know is that there are over a dozen bodies in
this building, some of which are unrecognizable lumps of

meat! You are the only person we found alive and YOU were found right in the middle of it! Now, what I want are some GODDAMN answers!!"

John never flinched during his tirade. Not when his chair crashed to the floor, nor when his hands slammed into the table, and he only sat and watched, stone-faced, until the other was finished.

"You shouldn't use HIS name in vain," John finally answered. "HE has a knack for punishing those who displease HIM."

"Jonesy? Could you please step outside?"

The voice over the speakers had spoken none too soon, as his right hand had begun balling into a fist. The two officers began moving forward to put a stop to anything that might happen, but it never got that far. Jonesy looked over his shoulder and growled through his teeth;

"I got this."

"Officer Jones. Please step outside immediately."

He turned and looked at John, who only blankly returned his stare, before storming from the room. From behind him, John heard the two men step back to their respective positions as one of them sighed in relief.

Several more minutes would pass before Officer Jones would return to the room. He quietly picked up his chair, scooted it back to the table and sat back down, returning his chin to the tops of his fists as he had done before.

"Religious man, are you?"

"No. Not anymore."

Jonesy cocked an eyebrow at his response.

"Oh, really? I happen to find that very interesting. You see, we found a whole lot of evidence that would suggest otherwise."

As he spoke, he raised his right hand and motioned for someone to enter from behind him. The gesture was answered within seconds as another officer entered the room carrying a transparent plastic tote filled with several items John immediately recognized. The tote was set down next to Officer Jones, who removed the top and began pulling the items out and laying them on the table before him.

"You recognize these, don't you," Jonesy asked as he moved his hands over John's possessions. He didn't answer right, following the other's hand as it passed over that which he had taken into battle with him; the bandoleer loaded with bolts for the hand crossbow. His dagger, the hand-guard and blade of which were intricately designed with holy symbols and names. His journal collection, as well as the bible handed down to him by his grandfather, all resting in a haphazard pile. Jessie and all of her ammunition, all of which were also intricately decorated with the sign of the cross, it was all there. Except, he didn't see the cross lying amongst his things.

"Want to tell me what happened to your hand there, Officer Jones?"

"I'll be asking the questions here, Mister Rizzerio," he answered a little more guiltily than he had intended. He had intentionally left the cross in the tote. There was something peculiar about it that he wanted to investigate when he had a little more time to himself.

"How is it that someone who has no religion comes across these kinds of things," he asked as he motioned to the items before him.

"This is a very peculiar set of tools you have here. If I didn't know any better, I'd say that you were—"

Jonesy's eyes widened, and he jerked backward in his chair, as a mental snapshot of the man dressed as Dracula flashed into his thoughts.

Nervously, one of the two officers spoke;

"Sir?"

His jaw slowly fell open as the pieces came together. This man was, IS, a vampire hunter! From across the table, John watched in bemused silence as the policeman came to the realization, and when their eyes next met, he only offered the slightest nod in answer.

Officer Jones began hurriedly putting John's things back into the tote, taking care to rewrap the journals and bible back in their protective cloths, and then motioned for the officer who brought it in to take it back out of the room. Once the tote and its bearer had left, he looked past the prisoner and at the two officers behind him.

"Leave us alone for a few minutes please."

"Sir?"

"DO IT!"

"Yes sir," they answered in unison. As they all but fled from the room, Jonesy stood and carried his chair around to John's side of the table, positioning it so that it was facing away from the windows, before sitting down.

Without turning to look at the prisoner, he quietly began to speak.

"Lower your head so that your hair covers your face." When he was satisfied that John wouldn't be seen speaking, he continued.

"When you answer me," he resumed in a near whisper, "keep your voice down so that the microphones can't pick it up. Got it?"

"Yeah. Sure thing, Officer Jones."

"Good. Now I want you to tell me about the real reason you were in that clothing store, and I also want to know why you needed silver weapons, wooden stakes, holy water, and the like."

Several moments of silence followed as John thought about how to best approach the subject. At one point he turned his head to study his captor, only to be ordered to face forward, and he found enough humor in the absurdity to elicit a smile. He had to know that anyone watching knew exactly what was going on, and furthermore, there wouldn't be enough time for a detailed story. The lawman cleared his throat impatiently at the precise moment that John decided to trust him with a short version. The worst that could happen would be imprisonment in a mental institution, after all.

"My name is John Rizzerio van Helsing," he began slowly, "and I am the last descendant of Abraham. I have walked the earth for over a century, pursuing the holy quest to destroy all things monstrous and evil to plague mankind, and until recently I championed the cause."

Jonesy's breath caught in his chest as he listened to him speak, and while it had to be the craziest thing he had ever heard, some part of him desperately needed to

65

believe it. After all, was it not just a few short hours ago that he looked upon this man's polar opposite; the vampire Tepes Vlad III? Was it not on the floor near his desk where the vampire enthralled his mind, seducing him into submission so that it may pass? And, wasn't there also something about this prisoner's cross? He shuddered as the memory eluded him and gasped after his body forced him to exhale the air he had been holding in.

This time it was his turn to look at the man next to him. Electricity seemed to fill the air between them, and he would later wonder if it hadn't originated from the man's words as he introduced himself for the first time.

"Eyes forward, Officer," John softly reminded him.

Jonesy snapped his attention to the wall at the back of the room as his mouth betrayed him, issuing forth his personal thoughts.

"Dear God, can it be true?"

"I'm afraid it is. When your men came upon me, it was after my friends and I had fallen in battle to the remaining forces of a vampire by the name of Draegan, a creature that had hunted my family for generations. At the exact moment that I had slain the foul creature, my best friends were stolen from me. One by kidnapping, the other, her life."

As the last sentence exited his mouth, it was John's turn to hitch in his breath. Tears leaked from the corners of his eyes as he spoke, and when he was finished, he buried his head into his hands.

"I failed them," he sobbed. "Jessie, Brody and Chloe, all dead because of my ego. And my family," he cried out. "They still have my wife and son!"

Jonesy's heart broke for this man. The pure emotion poured from the very center of his being and wrapped itself around the essence of the veteran officer, squeezing his soul with all of its angst and despair.

From behind him he could hear the door handle attempting to turn from the outside, but it wasn't opening. One of the two officers must have locked it on their way out! He made a mental note to personally buy them a drink after this was over, and wiped away the tears which had formed in the corner of his eyes.

"*Officer Jones? What's going on in there? Open this door*," shouted the tinny voice of his Captain from the speakers.

"One minute, ma'am," he answered smoothly before lowering his voice and speaking to the prisoner once more.

"Listen, we don't have much time. She's going to return to her office at any moment and get the key from her desk. We're only going to have a few moments, at best."

While he didn't remove his face from his hands, John nodded his understanding to what the man had said.

"I don't know why, but every instinct tells me to believe you. Not only that, but I should do everything in my power to help you as well."

John's head snapped up and he locked eyes with the man next to him, the latter of which who would gasp in astonishment before shakily continuing.

"I-if you'd given me that story before what had happened in containment this morning, I would have had you shipped off to the Looney bin. As it is, I still find it hard to swallow. But," he paused as he thought of how to proceed, "sometimes things happen for a reason."

As he was speaking, his hands absently began to remove the bandages from his left hand. They stuck to his skin from the blood that had leaked from his wounds, but peeled away painlessly.

"Near the end of the incident, someone, or rather, some THING appeared at the top of the steps the moment following the battering of the door. I don't recall doing it, but I must have reached into my desk, where I had stashed your cross, and grabbed ahold of it."

"Tell me," John spoke breathlessly, "what happened next?"

"I don't remember," he said after a moment of reflection, "but I have struggled with it in the hours since. Something about a light and the effect it had on the man at the top of the stairs, I think, but I can't be sure…"

"Hurry man," John gushed, reaching over to touch him lightly on the arm. "What happened next? It's important!"

"There was a hissing sound. No, that's not right. It was a shriek!"

The memories began to flood back after John touched him, and for the briefest moment he could feel the other's mind nudging his thoughts forward.

"Yes, it SHRIEKED," he cried as the door behind him burst open. "It shrieked, and what I saw was not a man! It was the biggest fucking snake I had ever seen! Except it was black and red! It had an open hood, much like a Cobra, and there were wings! It had wings on its back! THE DRAGON HAS COME, JOHN!!! HE'S COME FOR YOU!"

Terror once again filled the man's soul as the memory of what he had seen returned in full. His eyes bulged, and he began to gag as his stomach betrayed him. Turning quickly to the side, he bent over and vomited everything he had eaten earlier that night.

When the feeling finally passed, he noticed that something had changed about his left hand. He hadn't been aware that he had been removing the bandages; his hands had doing that on their own accord, and as he looked at the place where the wound had been, he saw the shape of the cross burned into the flesh of his palm. Only, it was no longer an injury. The wound had miraculously healed into pinkish colored scar tissue. Where the beams of the cross intersected was the face of the Christ, perfectly imprinted into his hand.

Just then, the door crashed open and Captain Haubbes led a small charge into the room. Three officers, none of whom had yet been in here, swept around the table with their guns drawn on the prisoner, while she closed in on her senior officer from the opposite side.

"Jonesy? Are you alright?"

He was openly weeping as he looked at something in his hand, and she couldn't remember ever being as terrified as she was at this exact moment.

"Lachlan," she spoke as calmly as could, "I need you to stand up and walk over to me, okay?"

"It's okay, Niki," he spoke between tears of joy, "it's going to be okay!"

68

"I know it is, Jonesy. Now, please. Please come around to this side of the table where we can talk about it?"

Jonesy looked once more into the golden-grey eyes of the man next to him, the very same eyes which moments before had seemed to glow softly around the edges, and John smiled in return as he lifted his fingers away from Jonesy's arm.

The silence was broken as, suddenly, one of the officers fired his weapon. The prisoner jumped in his seat once before slumping forward. As blood began to pool onto the table from beneath the cover of his auburn locks, Jonesy, who had ducked and covered his head when the shot rang out, looked up at the man next to him.

"Oh my god," he cried out in despair. "What have you DONE?!"

VII
A SHADOW OF DOUBT

Time continued to march on unnoticed in the darkness, and once again he awoke to the feeling of gentle swaying beneath him. At first he was disoriented. Recent events eluded his memory as he struggled out from beneath the shroud of sleep. He was curled up on the floor, covered in the soft shavings of some unknown substance, and his hands throbbed from the gentle reminder of the pain they had suffered.

His eyes slowly opened and a soft groan escaped him as he pulled himself into a sitting position. The air was fetid, rank with the mixture of death and the even fainter scent of vomit. From somewhere nearby he could hear something being broken. It is a wooden, rhythmic cracking sound, not unlike that of a tree limb breaking beneath the weight of snow, followed by an insidious crunching.

A shiver traversed the length of his spine, beginning at the short hairs on the back of his neck, and ending somewhere behind his stomach. His every instinct screamed that something was terribly wrong, but for some reason his mind had locked away his most recent memories.

A soft light glows from somewhere outside of his prison, shining in from high above, and gently trickling through an opening just a few inches before him. A tendril of fear reaches out and wraps its icy hands around his heart as he leans forward to discover its source. A light sweat breaks out on his forehead and he begins to tremble from the anxiety of what he might find.

Try as he might, however, it was against his nature to fight the urges propelling him forward. It was as much curiosity, as it was the need to learn, that drove him to seek the answer to this puzzle, and he was helpless to deter from his course of action. For whatever inexplicable reason, he just HAD to see what was responsible for the noises outside.

His nose pressed against the rough wooden surface of the wall before him, while his eyes peered through the

70

three inch tall opening. The ominous crunching
continued from somewhere below, but nothing was visible
from his vantage. He was able to see that the source of
the light originated from a moonbeam shining through a
skylight from somewhere above. Unable to complete its
journey to the floor, it filtered into a large crystal
vase on a shelf just across from him. The effect was an
iridescent glow that, while pretty to look at, did
nothing to chase away the darkness around it.

He huffed as he sat back against the wall behind him.
It was just as well. The smell of vomit was strongest
by the opening, the latter of which was pungent with the
rich scent of putrefaction that wafted into the confines
of his small space. His prison lurched from his
movement, the gentle swaying suddenly becoming erratic,
and he placed his palms against the walls in order to
prevent himself from sliding around.

Several minutes would pass before he felt comfortable
enough to lay his hands back into his lap, and before
the swaying would return to normal. During that time he
focused his considerable mental abilities toward finding
some answers. His mind still would not allow him to
know what had led up to this moment, so he focused on
what was currently going on around him instead.

His prison was a small wooden crate, approximately
3'w X 4'l X 3'd, the inside of which the bottom was
layered with soft pine shavings. He had recently been
sick to his stomach. He not only smelled it from the
right corner beneath the opening, but the smell was on
him as well. His head ached from a recent injury and
his hands were so battered that the only way to
comfortably hold them was curled in his lap, with the
palms facing upward, and his fingers pointing toward his
chin.

The moonlight was an obvious indicator that it was
still night, but it couldn't have been the same night
that he and his friends had last been together. A
terrible thirst burned in the center of his abdomen, and
his lips were dry and cracked from lack of moisture.
Even the light sweat that had been on his forehead had
soaked back into his thirsty pores. His stomach gurgled
hungrily as well. He had never gone more than a few

71

hours without eating something, as he had always been a nervous eater, and it had been years since he could last remember feeling the pain of hunger so strongly inside of him.

He watched the beam of moonlight sway back and forth before the opening and listened to the gentle creaking that followed each time it reached the farthest edge. Unlike some of the other crates outlined by the pale light, his was suspended above the ground by some form of rope or pulley system that was somehow secured from the sides of his prison, as well as from above. This would explain why he only seemed to sway forward to back without making rotations, and for that he was thankful.

While he had been exploring the interior of his prison, the sounds from outside had ceased. Whatever was in the darkness below had either gotten its fill, or lost interest in the meal that it was working on, and had since moved onto something else. What that could possibly be, would remain a mystery another light source chased more of the darkness away.

"You're awake," a raspy voice spoke from somewhere below. "I can tell by the sound of your breathing, and the fear that you are feeling, that you must truly be, awake."

He had been concentrating so intently, listening for any sound below, that the speaker had startled him into crying out.

"Fear not. I have had my fill. I will not harm you."

The speaker sighed contently before continuing.

"The master seems to think you are very important," it said inquisitively. "I cannot say why. You stink of righteousness."

"I-I don't u-understand," he answered. "Are y-you the A-albino?"

The raspy voice cackled with amusement for several moments before continuing.

"No. That one and I are much, much different."

"W-what are you?"

"I am the end of the food chain, the Omega, and it is I that disposes of that which is left behind."

There was a short intake of breath before the speaker continued.

"You should worry more about yourself, little one. The master will be calling for you soon."

"W-who is this m-master you speak of?"

The Omega continued as if it hadn't heard him.

"Nobody has ever been called to the master, and returned to tell the tale."

The volume of the Omega's voice began to get more distant with each word, as if it were moving away while it spoke.

"W-wait! I have m-more questions to a-ask you!"

"I'm tired, and my belly is full. I will allow you one more question before I must return to my slumber. Speak, human. Ask quickly before I lose my patience with you."

"Y-your master… W-what is your m-master's name?"

The Omega snorted.

"You will find out soon enough. I wouldn't be so eager to know the name of that one. He is much worse than either I, or the Albino combined."

The raspy voice faded, leaving behind an eerie void in its wake. He hadn't realized he had been doing it at the time, but during the exchange he had leaned forward as he tried to see the image of the 'other', which had been near his prison. His knees ached in protest when he scooted back, and he pulled his feet out from under him in an effort to find some comfort in his small area of confinement.

Slowly, he drew his knees up to his chest and laid his head against them in defeat. His body ached from the recent abuse it had taken, and he wanted nothing more than an escape from it all. He closed his eyes and wrapped his arms tightly around his legs, trying to pull himself as far into himself as physically possible, so that he may further block out the reality around him, and he began to cry.

His tears fell, brought by the fear for his situation. They were hot, bitter tears that quickly soaked into his parched skin, which left him feeling more ill than good. He wept silently, his chest hitching painfully with each sob, and he continued until his tear ducts had no more moisture left to offer.

It was then that he came to the realization; he was utterly alone. There was nobody left to rescue him from the evil lurking outside his prison. Brody, whom he had depended heavily upon in J.R.'s absence, had been senselessly torn murdered at their last campsite. For all he knew, Chloe had fallen to her attackers at *The Clothing Store,* and J.R. hadn't survived his battle against Draegan. There was nobody for him to turn to for help. Not even Jessie, whose disappearance and eventual death had led up to this very moment.

He succumbed to his sadness and wept until the moonlight passed out of range of the skylight, finally plunging him in complete darkness.

Sometime later, as he rested apathetically after his emotional release, he realized he could see several dark shapes emerging from the shadows. Slowly, he once again leaned forward and peeked through the opening. He saw increasingly more of the room by the light of the coming sun, and that the shapes belonged to steel shelves just across from where he was suspended.

Peering up through the skylight, he could see a hint of orange creeping into the heavens, and his thoughts returned once more to the morning after they had discovered their fallen companion.

His arms ached from the efforts of the last two hours. He and John had trudged through the wild, hauling stones from the creek bed, to build a cairn over their friend. He trembled from exhaustion, each step taking twice as much effort as the last, but he wouldn't allow himself to be slowed down.

Just a little off to his side, John walked sullenly, with his head bent down and hair hanging loosely around his face. He had removed his duster and left it at the clearing, wrapped around Chloe's shoulders, and his arms bulged from the load of stones that he was carrying.

Neither had said a word since they had begun laying their friend to rest, and he desperately wished he could think of something to say. As heavy as own heart was, he could see the pain literally radiating from his formerly indestructible companion.

While Chloe had openly taken it the hardest of the three, Quinn saw in John what his own heart had felt at the discovery. He saw the spirit of the hunter breaking.

"J-john," he asked at one point. His friend had only slightly slowed his pace to show that he was listening.

"A-are we g-gonna be alright?"

John didn't answer the question with words. As he picked up the pace on their trek back to the clearing, Quinn saw a single tear fall from the left eye of his friend, and suddenly he was very afraid.

No other exchange was made between the two, and after returning to the clearing with the final stones, they went about the grim task of moving and burying their friend. John showed a great amount of respect for the remains, wrapping it tightly with a blanket before he and Quinn moved it to its final resting place. Chloe listlessly set about fashioning a grave marker using the laces from his boots and two pieces of wood from the forest floor.

During the time that it taken for them to prepare the grave, Chloe hadn't once looked at their brutish friend's remains. She couldn't bring herself to do it, after seeing the horror on the faces of her companions, and she wanted to remember him as she had last seen him. After thrusting the marker into the dirt at the foot of the grave, she desperately sought the grey-gold eyes of her mentor and implored upon him.

"How did he die John?"

Both she and Quinn expected the answer, and when he finally gave it to them, both could feel the presence of evil closing around them like a vice.

"Draegan," was the simple answer, and yet, the feelings that it evoked in all of them were not simple at all. They were defeated before they had begun. The creature had not only been watching them, but it was somehow stalking them as well, and there was no telling how long it had been doing so. But then again, it didn't really matter anymore. The vampire had taken from them their hope in Jessie, their pillar of strength

*in Brody, and it had severely damaged their spirit in
the process.*

*They spent the day in the clearing, telling stories
about their friend until they hadn't the strength to
continue. When evening finally approached, they said
their goodbyes to their friend, each of them knowing
that they would never return to this spot again.*

*Solemnly, they returned to the campsite. No words
were spoken between the three as they climbed into their
vehicles; John and Chloe in the Impala, and Quinn in the
Mustang. Soon they were roaring along the highway with
the Impala once more in the lead.*

It was the look in John's eyes that had stuck with
him. He had known that look intimately, as it was that
very same feeling of defeat that haunted him for so many
years of his life. John had come into his life and
rescued him from that feeling, giving him the hope that
he could truly live outside the confines of his home.
His heart was heavy with the loss of their friend, but
to see the haunted look of despair settling into John's
eyes was just too much to bear.

As he hunkered in the shadows of the warehouse,
waiting for dawn to come, he found that he had plenty of
time to think about that lonely trek back to camp. He
had seen more than despair in the eyes of his friend
that morning. There had been something else there as
well. For the first time since he had met him, John had
looked weary.

It was something that had never occurred to him over
the years. In all the time that he had known him, he
had never once thought about the emotional baggage that
must come with the burden John carried. By J.R.'s own
words, he had been around for longer than any of them
had even been alive. Because he was the chosen heir to
the 'van Helsing legacy', he wasn't allowed to move on
until he was succeeded by an heir of his own blood, or
of his choosing.

He couldn't imagine the horrors that John must have
lived through in all that time, and not just the recent
events over the last twenty years, but with everything
that he had ever been through up to this point. Even

before waking up in his prison, he knew by John's words alone that there were other creatures out there than the vampires that they had set out to defeat. In one of their most recent conversations, John had hinted the existence of zombies. In a conversation he'd had with him several years ago, he had also spoken of the existence of lycanthropes as well.

God only knew how many other creatures were out there fighting on the other side. Well, God and John Rizzerio van Helsing, anyways. He had never pried much into the world of the supernatural, not wanting to know more than John had allowed him to, and he had only conducted research on that which was needed, AS it was needed.

His mind was working in overdrive, and as a result, everything that had happened to him since first waking in this box came rushing back. The changing of the albino had shocked him so much that he must have blocked its memory, but now that he remembered it, he was only presented with even more questions.

He wished that he had access to a library or a computer so that he could research for the answers he needed. Unconsciously, he patted his breast pocket for his notepad and pen. The action was purely by instinct, and when he realized it still wasn't there, he sighed and dropped his hand back to his lap.

"Why d-didn't it reveal itself b-before," he quietly asked himself. The question answered itself in its speaking as he suddenly recalled that the albino had transformed into a Jackal. If he remembered correctly, Jackals were carrion feeders because they were cowards at heart.

"W-why then," he wondered silently. Why then, did it reveal itself to him now? It was a difficult question, and the only answer that he could think of was that they hadn't had enough exposure to the creature. Perhaps, even, its nature had kept it hidden from them as well. Unlike a wolf, which would gladly charge into battle for its Alpha, the jackal had chosen to orchestrate events from behind the scenes.

As he contemplated the events from earlier that evening, the pieces to another puzzle began to shift into place. His eyes widened when he realized that

there was no way that Draegan could have been personally
responsible for what happened back at the camp. When
they went into battle at the store, the initial vampires
had moved much faster than their human opponents, but
not so much that his party couldn't track their
movements. Draegan wouldn't have been able to kill
their friend and cross the centennial number of miles
between the rest stop and *The Clothing Store* before the
coming dawn. If he had driven, they would have heard
his approach the night before. They had been far enough
from civilization that they would have heard its
approach long before they had seen it.

The more he thought about it, the more he believed
that it wasn't a vampire which was responsible for what
happened to Brody as well. When they had found him, he
lay several feet away from his arm, which had been torn
completely from its socket. He had crawled the distance
from his arm to the fallen tree, mostly dead from blood
loss, and had scrawled his final message before the
attacker had finished what it had started. It had
watched, with cold and calculating eyes, as Brody
scrawled his bloody apology, before doing what it had
been sent to do.

The attack on Brody had been brutal, but it wasn't
the kind of attack one would associate with a vampire.
What had been done to him had come from something more
primal then the upper intelligence normally associated
with the type of undead they were hunting. This had
been bestial and so full of rage that even their strong
friend hadn't stood a chance.

His fingers twitched reflexively on his right hand,
scrawling at a notepad that he no longer had, and he
fell deep into his thoughts for the next several
moments. Outside his container, the sunrise continued
to shine in all of its majesty upon the warehouse,
illuminating it with its fiery splendor and revealing
everything as it had been before being covered by the
darkness of night.

Beneath the roof of the warehouse was a maze of steel
shelving, each of which were filled with wooden crates.
No two crates are the same size, nor is the wood
fashioned from the same species of tree. Just as the

crates varied in size, so too did they in color as well. Some are fashioned from White Oak, while others could easily be Brazilian Walnut.

Over sixty thousand square feet of the warehouse was occupied by the maze of shelving, but there are two areas left completely clean. Near the center of the building and slightly closer to the back, is an area that has been made especially for working with whatever was being put in, or taken out of, the containers. It is an almost perfectly shaped oval clearing, when looked upon from above, and contains three large worktables. On a shelf under each of the tables is a small area for placing tools, though some have been scattered haphazardly across the floor.

There is also a small break area off to one side, in which two card tables are butted together. Eight chairs surround these, and there are playing cards and empty beer bottles scattered, forgotten, across their surface. A small refrigerator and snack machine sit just a few feet away, as well as a small table with a microwave, underneath of which is a shelf with paper plates, cups and plastic silverware with which to eat.

Near the back of the work area is a small metal desk, used mostly for paperwork. If one had visited during normal operating hours, they would be hard pressed to tell something were amiss. However, the area had changed quite a bit in the last week and a half. Suspended directly over the ruins of the work area is a large crate, inside of which Quinn is currently trying to mentally process all of the details of his last few hours. The metal desk is covered by a crusted pool of dried blood, very much like several small areas around the floor of the clearing.

There are no longer any bodies, however. Only the rusty stains they had left behind suggest that something had gone terribly wrong here. Several crates had been moved into one corner where, not too long ago a worker had been crushed, and are in various states of disrepair. A few are riddled with bullet holes, while others are completely dismantled piles of wood.

An arrow of light, fired from the chariot of Apollo, launches through a skylight near the back of the warehouse, chasing away the remaining shadows and revealing the only other area not filled with shelving. Mostly empty at the moment, this area was currently being used for parking. A bay door, large enough for a Semi, opens from here to the outside. There is also a small shipping office, inside of which the lights are currently shut off.

Back inside the crate, Quinn mentally files away his most recent findings and sighs at not having his usual means to record them. Just as he isn't aware that his hand is absently scrawling his notes down, with a pen it doesn't hold, into a notebook that isn't there, so too is he not aware of the sunlight as it begins to explore the inside of the warehouse. Nor does he notice his cell phone sitting in the pine shavings near his feet. He doesn't notice when the screen suddenly comes to life, with the message; Incoming call From J.R., and he doesn't see when the battery depleted message warns him of the imminent power down just seconds before his phone powers off.

It wasn't until the sun had pulled itself triumphantly over the horizon that he would again become aware of his surroundings. He returned from his thoughts with no more answers to his questions, than when he had turned into them, and he slumped back with a frustrated sigh. There had to be some connection to what had happened to Brody, Jessie, Emily and Bran, but he couldn't find it! Angrily, he balled his right hand into a fist and punched the palm of his left, sending a flare of pain so brilliant up his arms that he yelped in agony.

"S-stupid," he cursed himself.

They had all thought that Draegan had been the root of all their woes, but try as he might, he couldn't find the connection. Of everything that he knew about vampire lore, as well as that which John had corrected for his benefit, nothing seemed to add up. If Draegan had taken J.R.'s family, as they had assumed that he had, why then was the battle so anticlimactic? There was never any mention of their names by either the Albino or Draegan. If they had taken them, wouldn't it have been wiser to use them against J.R. in hopes of causing him to err in battle?

He had known J.R. for most of his adult life. It wasn't until recently that he had been brought into the world of the supernatural.

"N-no, t-that isn't r-right," Quinn muttered softly.

He and John had spoken for years about the supernatural. Being a bookworm particularly fond of the great works of fiction, he had quite an extensible knowledge of creatures that most would not. It was through his book dealer that J.R. would learn of him and eventually make the visit that would forever change his outlook on life.

They'd spent several weeks together, each visit subtly initiated by a question designed to peak his interest at a moment before he had to leave. Eventually they grew to be great friends, and J.R. would coax him out of his home and into a world that he had left years behind. The rest, as they say, become quickly become history.

J.R. eventually let him in on his secret, but not as openly as he had done in the hotel room with Brody. As their friendship grew, they spoke more often, sharing their diverse educations with one another. While J.R. helped him to overcome his fear of the world, he also came to him with questions that were designed to dig through his own expansive learning. He used Quinn's insight to ease him out into the world, so that while he was answering John's questions, he would completely lose track of where he was. It was a good ploy. He would finish speaking about something only to realize that he was a little farther away from his comfort zone. Eventually, his fear vanished altogether, with the only remaining affect being his stutter.

"You have to hurry, Q-man. You're running out of time."

His thoughts jumped back into the present, and he was startled to hear the ghostly voice of his friend interrupting his reverie.

"I-I don't k-know what to d-do," he cried out in frustration.

"It's like I always tell ya, little buddy. You've got to finish what you've started."

"But I c-can't! M-my hands h-hurt so much," he sobbed.

There was nothing further from Brody, and after ten minutes he began to feel the slightest shadow of doubt he had ever heard anything at all. It was more likely that beyond his pain, past his hunger, and at the limits of his thirst, his mind was creating hallucinations in order to nudge him into action.

Nevertheless, he crawled up to his knees and placed his eyes against the opening, squinting against the light of the morning sun as he struggled to determine the height of his prison. He knelt that way for some time, longer than most Catholics would during mass, but finally his vision began to clear. Details swam into focus and he was able to roughly determine his prison being around seven to ten feet in the air.

His thoughts traveled to the sounds from the night before, when he saw the blood stains below, and he shuddered in revulsion. Whatever he had been speaking to had disposed of the bodies by-

"eating them," he finished with disgust.

At that moment his stomach gurgled hungrily and he glanced down with a look of irritation.

"Y-you sure p-pick a funny t-time to remind m-me," he grumbled back.

As the last of his words are spoken, his eyes widen and he sits backward with a thump, recalling the voices that spoke outside his prison just before he had knocked out the board. The more experienced of the two had meant for the subordinate to feed and water him without opening the crate!

He shoved his hands down into the pine shavings and quickly searched for what he knew had to be there. A large splinter from the bottom of the crate jammed its way beneath the fingernail on the middle finger of his right hand, but he hardly flinched. Without a giving it a second thought, he yanked it out and continued his search.

"...hurry!"

82

"D-damn it Brody," he cursed, "I-I'm doing t-the b-best I can!"

After searching the walls next to him and behind him with no luck, he focused his attention to the wall in front of him. His hands slid forward, his right lightly bumping his cell phone in passing, until they came to stop against a loose panel several inches below the opening he had already made.

When pushing it outward proved to be unsuccessful, he sat back and thought about what to do next.

"W-what if-" he asked to himself, as an idea suddenly came into existence. It was a fairly good idea, but he would later wish that he had put more thought into it before putting it into action.

Quickly, he turned himself around until his back was against the wall with the opening, slid down enough to give his legs room to work and then pumped them out against the wall he had spent most of his time leaning against.

Behind him, the already weakened wall creaked as its nails slid out of the boards on either side of him. He felt it beginning to give, but leave enough time for him to act on it. He was so desperate to be free of his confinement that he now acted purely on instinct. Even as the wall began to fall away behind him, he pumped out with his legs, kicking with all that he had left to give.

Seconds later, he watched in confusion as the crate he had just exited, floated farther away from him with each agonizingly slow second that followed. Bits of pine shavings rained out of the opening of the structure, those nearest him clumped together with the substances that had been his last meal, followed by a black rectangular object which he would later realize was his phone.

He didn't have any more time to think about it, however, as at that moment he hit the floor below hard enough to knock the air from his lungs and send him spiraling back to the edge of unconsciousness.

VIII

NO ESCAPE FROM REALITY

"Get yur ass up, boy! It's time for yur lesson."

John rubbed his eyes vigorously with the palms of his hands as he aggressively tried to chase the sleep away. Slowly, he sat up and looked across the small room to the bed where his sister slept, only to see that it was already empty. This didn't surprise him at all, however, as she almost never seemed to need as much sleep as he did.

Their shared room was bare, consisting of only the essentials needed to live in. Each had their own bed, his being against the southern wall, while hers was against the northern wall. Their possessions fit in a small locker at the foot of their beds, and each shared a large dresser centered on the eastern wall. It was behind him that he heard his grandfather's gruff call and he knew better than to slouch when summoned.

Moving quickly, he rummaged through his drawers until he found something warm enough to stave off the morning air, dressed, and left the room. The living area was empty and he could hear his family already hard at work outside of their small home.

"Come on out here boy," Aedesius called to him. "Time's a wastin'!"

It was still dark outside and he shivered when the crisp morning air eagerly greeted him at the door. He was thankful, however, to see that they had built a small fire by which to train by. Not only would there be enough light, but it would give them some much needed warmth as well. While it was still technically the summer season, mornings were growing much colder with autumn fast on its heels.

"Quit your gawking and git down here already!"

He wasted no time, running to where his family was already hard at work. As he approached, Aedesius tossed him a sheathed silver dagger which he caught without breaking stride, and motioned for him to take his usual position. The techniques they learned were simple, each repeated in sets of one hundred, and all were designed to defend or to disarm the opponent. They trained well into the morning, he with the silver dagger and Jessie with a blade which had supposedly come from somewhere in the Far East. Unlike his, which was straight and narrowed to a point, the blade of hers was curved, with only the sharp edge narrowing to a tip.

Hours later, lunch time found the two siblings near exhaustion, and their grandfather watching them sympathetically, as they sat together on the front steps.

"Grandfather," Jessie asked. "Why must we get up so early to train?"

"Because, my dear child," he answered solemnly, "that which I am training you to fight against never sleeps."

It was the most explanation that he had given since taking them in, and it brought them no closer to understanding. He left them to rest where they were, as he went inside to prepare lunch, and Jessie laid her head wearily upon her brother's shoulder.

"I wish we could just play," she whispered softly.

"I know, but grandfather says-"

"Pshh," she interrupted, pushing angrily away from him. "He says a lot of things, but nothing ever makes any sense. Why are we up before the sun every day, training to defend ourselves against an enemy which we have no name for?"

He had no answers for her questions, however. He never did. These were frequent questions they had shared with one another since shortly after arriving, and the answers didn't seem to be getting any closer.

"I dunno, but whatever it is, I'm pretty sure he's afraid of it."

She slowly nodded her head in agreement and looked out to the edge of the property where the tree line began.

"I really miss them, you know," she said after a few minutes.

"Yeah, I know. I do too."

"Why doesn't anyone tell us what happened to them?"

Her voice cracked slightly with the question, and as she choked back the familiar feeling of sadness that came when talking of their parents, her eyes glistened from the tears that formed at their edges.

"It has to be because of our age, I think," he offered rather lamely. "Whatever it was must have been-"

"...horrible," Aedesius finished from behind them. They both jumped at the sound of his voice, but he didn't take much notice. He looked over them and to the trees, just as Jessie had moments before.

"You need not worry about that, not just yet. For now, I want you two to run over to the well and wash yur selves up for lunch."

"Yes sir," both answered in unison. They only paused long enough to look at each other and giggle for having spoken at the same time.

Before eating, as was quickly becoming tradition in their new home, they joined hands and said a brief prayer. There was nothing special about it. It was a simple "Our Father...", but it was upon their grandfather's insistence that they said it before every meal.

They ate in silence, each mostly to their own thoughts. Their meal consisted of wild boar, which had been roasted the day before, and vegetables from the garden. It had been a good season for growing and the larder was overflowing with the extra food that had been preserved for the coming winter.

John ate hungrily, shoveling food in as fast as he could swallow it, while his sister listlessly poked at hers.

"What's the matter with ya then," their elder finally asked. "I didn't hear ya complainin' yesterday about my cookin'".

"It's nothing grandfather," she answered halfheartedly.

"Don't give me that now. Yur obviously thinking about something now, or you'd be cleaning that plate like yur bruther there."

"It's just that-"

Aedesius looked across the table impatiently and motioned for her to continue.

"Well, I'm bored. WE'RE bored! When we arrived here, we were only given a week to grieve. But what exactly ARE we grieving, anyway? We were only told that

86

our parents had died, and the most we have even been told is that it was horrible! Every day that we've been here, we have tended the garden. We've fetched water from the well and we've cleaned your home from top to bottom. Six out of seven days we are up before the sun, training to do battle with someone whom we have no knowledge of. Why, grandfather?! Why do you teach us these things and not tell us why we must know them?"

As she spoke, her voice rose and her temper flared until she finished near a fevered pitch. During this time, John's face darkened with the same anger and frustration she was feeling as well. His eating slowed until, when she finally finished, he was no longer reaching for the food before him, and he too, turned their shared feelings unto their elder.

"Not only that," he added as calmly as he could, "but why must we always stay on the property? Why is there never any time for us to play? Whenever we have free time, we're supposed to use it for more work, rather than doing the things that we should be doing."

When they had finished, Aedesius calmly reached into his lap and took hold of the cloth napkin he kept there during meals. He didn't have much use for silverware, as it was just one more thing for thieves to steal or for him to wash, but he did insist that anyone sitting at his table use a napkin. Quietly, he wiped the grease from his hands without looking at either of the children and placed the napkin on top of his uneaten food.

He then stood and walked from the kitchen and into the main living room. With his back still to them, he softly offered more mystery with his only answer.

"When you are finished, please clean up and join me on the porch."

Both siblings looked at one another for several moments as they listened to their grandfather walk first into his room, rustle some things around, and finally re-enter the living room to then exit the cabin.

"I'll clean up the dishes if you take care of the food," Jessie finally offered as she pushed her plate across to him.

"You need to eat," he protested.

"I do eat, John, just not as much as you. Quit being such a worry-wart."

He looked down at her plate and noticed that she had cleared most of the vegetables away, leaving only a couple bites of carrots and all of her meat.

"It's not healthy to just eat vegetables Jess," he protested grumpily. There wasn't as much strength behind his argument, however, as he very rarely turned down any meat when it was offered to him. She only chuckled as she wrapped the rest of the uneaten food and put it away for the next meal. This was an argument they'd had several times before, and it wasn't one that he was going to win in the near future.

John watched his sister while she cleaned and marveled at how alike they were. When they had lived in the city, they had spent very little time together. Their parents had sent them to private schools when they were old enough, and they had only seen each other for the holidays or during break.

She was an exact model of him, only more feminine. He had heard somewhere that male and female twins were impossible, but here was proof that it was only improbable. He had known that they were unique early on, and not just because of their shared appearance.

"You're thinking about us again, aren't you," she asked coyly from across the room.

His face flushed as he nearly choked on the bite of food he was chewing on. She only laughed and threw her arms around him on her way past to put the iron skillet away, pressing her cheek against his.

"It's okay. I promised I wouldn't do it anymore, didn't I?"

The 'it' that she was speaking of was an uncanny ability they seemed to share with one another. Whenever they were together, they were able to impart upon the other their emotional states. This wasn't uncommon amongst identical twins, but it was what they could do when apart that was scary. By concentrating hard enough, they could send the other a mental image of what they were seeing, or of something they wanted the other to see. Jessie had even claimed that she had once been able to hear his thoughts as well!

As if she was reading him at that moment, she squeezed one final time before moving away to finish cleaning.

"What do you think he's gonna tell us" he asked between bites."

"I don't know. I just hope it's something that we can handle."

"We can handle anything as long as we stick together, sis. We've made it this far haven't we?"

They finished in silence and when he had cleaned both his and her plates, he helped her clean and put the rest of the dishes away before they joined their grandfather on the porch. It had been a good hour since they had finished their lessons and eaten. They both noticed this immediately from the positioning of the sun.

"Over here," their grandfather hollered from the northern side of the house. They followed the sound of his voice to the end of the porch, where he was laying out several items on a large tree stump that he affectionately called 'The Round Table.'

It had been there for years, quite possibly since before the property had been cleared out, and had since been leveled off and shellacked for use as a table. Around it were several smaller stumps that had received a similar treatment for use as seats. It wasn't very often that he had anyone sit with him at 'The Round Table', and it had been years since it was last used, but this afternoon would see it full of activity once more.

They gave one another a puzzled expression when they saw the items that he had lain out. Some of what they saw was familiar, while other pieces they had never in all their time at that cabin.

"Sit," he said as they approached.

"What is all of this," John asked inquisitively.

"You'll know soon enough," he answered gruffly. "Now, yur sure ya want the answers to yur questions, right."

It was more of a statement, than a question, and both only nodded their affirmation as they waited for him to continue.

89

"You two are very special, more so than you realize. Not only are you twins, but you were born identical twins of opposite gender. Now, to my knowledge, not only did you beat the odds just by being twins, but you completely stepped around them when you came as one of each.

And, that isn't the end of it. There's so much more about ya that you two need to know. I had hoped that ya would be much older before we had this discussion, but I can see how strong yur values are. You ought to be proud, you two, yur parents taught you well."

He motioned impatiently for them to have a seat and waited until they were comfortable before continuing. He drew their attention to three items, placing each before them and encouraging them to handle each one respectively.

The first was a wooden cross. The wood was a dark, roughly cut species that they puzzled over for several minutes. Jessie handled it first, turning it over in her hands and admiring the work. Upon the cross is a very lifelike Jesus, crucified by his wrists and feet. Every detail stands out on his body, from the final spear thrust to the lacerations inflicted upon him prior to his being nailed to the cross.

His eyes were closed, but his face was frozen with a look of serene peacefulness that seemed to radiate onto those looking at him. Where the nails were driven into the flesh of the Christ are small droplets of blood. She gingerly reached out and touched them, amazed that it actually came away from the marble skin of the savior.

"John," she uttered breathlessly as she showed it to him.

Aedesius watched this exchange very closely. He knew the true secret to the choosing of the heir, and only the next moment would reveal to him the answer.

John reached for the cross, eager to examine the bleeding artifact for himself. It lay face up on the palm of his sister's left hand and the only natural way to grab it was below the Christ's feet, but even so, it was only their grandfather who noticed when the statue's eyes fluttered open and looked upon the young boy.

90

The moment was fleeting. If he hadn't known what to look for he could have written it off as his imagination, but this wasn't the case. Long ago, his father had told him of the first time he had held the artifact. He remembered how, in the story, the eyes of the savior had opened and it had spoken to him.

While the latter hadn't happened when he was chosen, nor was it going to happen this day as well, he was to be the one to know the heir had been chosen. The eyes of the Lord were as blue as the ocean and surrounded by a ring of gold. To look too long into his eyes was to invite the taint of madness, for those eyes held all of eternity within them; something that the average mortal couldn't comprehend. The golden ring appeared smoky, with varying shades of gold swirling around the majestic blue orbs of the Christ. There was depth to them and, for that briefest of seconds, he saw the gates of heaven somewhere beyond that golden mist.

The moment passed. The Christ had looked upon the young boy, had made the next heir apparent, and its eyes had closed once more. John, however, hadn't seen this. His attention had been focused on the signs of dogma being presented to him from the artifact.

"What does it mean, grandfather," he quietly asked.

Aedesius only took the cross from him as he set the next item before them. It was a small, leather bound book. The material was worn and fraying in several places. The pages, loose and facing several different directions, were stuffed almost carelessly inside. The book was held closed by two bright red ribbons, one running from the spine to the outer edge, while the other ran from the top to bottom.

Jessie, whom of the two had the strongest affinity for books, was the first to reach forward. Just as reverently as she had handled the cross, she lifted the book, examining at great length before untying the ribbons. She opened it somewhere near the middle to the page of a creature that had a very reptilian look to it. It was only a facial profile, but the drawing itself was very detailed. While it had a human shape, there were only holes where the nose should be. It had a pronounced ridge over its eyes, the latter of which were

91

yellow, vertical slits. Its mouth was slightly open, in the darkness of which two fangs could be seen pointing downward and a forked tongue flickered from within.

The words around the drawing were nothing like anything she had seen before, and with a frown, she passed the book to her brother.

John looked further into the book and came across two other drawings that were just as detailed and twice as disturbing as the first. One was of a man who was in mid-transformation as it shifted into the form of a doglike creature. The other was also of a man, but it was drawn with horrific wounds on its body. The eyes were cold, inhuman, and it appeared to be eating something that looked suspiciously like another person's arm.

By the time he had finished looking at the third drawing his sister had set the next item down in front of him. It was something he was very familiar with, but something that he had not seen before in their home. Lying before him was a small, wooden mallet. The handle was twice as long as his hands, when made into fists and set one over the other, and he could see words that were scrawled in the same language as was found in the book.

"...in lege Domini voluntas eius..."

The head of the mallet was frayed, stained with something dark and sinister, and when he examined it closely he could see the image of a cross burnt upon it.

"I don't understand," he said. "Why are you showing us these things?"

There were several other items to look at; small vials containing clear liquid and with crosses etched into their stoppers, several wooden stakes, a small bundle wrapped in black cloth, his training dagger and a hacksaw all lay before them.

Aedesius didn't answer for several moments. He was lost in thought. There was a dark expression on his face, and the fact that he seemed to be staring through his grandchildren made them more than a little uncomfortable. Though they squirmed beneath his frightful scrutiny, they said nothing knowing that he would speak when he was ready. That moment finally came a few minutes later, but not before he blinked his eyes and looked off into the woods behind them, as he had from the front porch.

"These are tools that were handed down from my father," he began deliberately. "With the exception of the cross, each is the work of his and my own hands, designed to kill the creatures you saw in that book."

The afternoon grew long as he spoke to them about the creatures they had seen, as well as a few they had not. He spoke to them of the purpose of the tools that lay before them and of tools that he didn't yet have. Most importantly, he spoke of the cross, of their destiny and about the importance of their isolation.

They spoke long into the night, stopping only to relieve themselves, and once to further demolish the leftovers of their previous meal. They listened with the patience of monks, conversed with the wisdom of adults, and it was on that day when they lost their innocence, thus beginning their journey down the road to becoming hunters.

It would nearly be sunrise when they would finally finish the first of many 'Round Table' discussions, and after picking up, they wandered off to their respective beds. John shivered as he thought about how their lives had so quickly changed. He was destined to battle the devil's creatures? It all seemed like such madness, and it was something that he would have to work on understanding if he was going to believe it.

He trembled slightly and pulled his blanket up to his nose. He could smell the strong scent of the campfire hanging on his clothes, but there was no more warmth to be had. Now, away from the fire and in the confines of their cabin, which hadn't burned a fire in the fireplace throughout this night, he could feel the cold morning air reaching in and massaging him to the bone. He wished for another blanket, but he had given that to Jess a few nights back when she had been in a similar predicament.

Eventually, he was able to drift off to sleep, and when he did, his dreams were plagued with the likes of vampires, werewolves and several other creatures that he had learned of that day. He slept well past breakfast, and it wouldn't be until after lunch when his growling stomach, and the light from the outside, would wake him.

The cabin was eerily silent, and like the morning before, he awakened to discover that he was alone. Worried more about quelling the hunger inside his belly, he left his room still wearing the clothes from the day before and wandered to the pantry. The cabin remained quiet, and after eating a piece of bread and salted meat, he went in search of his family.

Much like the cabin had been, the property was also quiet. There were no sounds of training, nor could he hear the voices of his grandfather or sister. With the exception of the sounds that normally filled the air, nothing disturbed the small clearing.

"Must be off hunting," he muttered.

He stretched the sleep from his muscles and spent the next hour going through some of his daily exercises. They weren't something that he would have been doing the previous year, but then again, he was no longer the same child he was before. Ever since coming to live here, his grandfather had been grooming him, conditioning him, for what lie ahead. The year previous would have found a much more innocent John in a school house, learning the ways of the world, but here, they were learning the ways of a world that existed beneath.

When he finished with exercises that would become a morning ritual for years to come, he drew a bucket of water from the well and drank several ladles worth before pouring the rest over his head. It was then that he noticed his sister sitting at The Round Table. He hadn't been able to see her from the front of the cabin earlier, but the well allowed for him to easily see around the north and south sides of the cabin.

She was leaning over a book, her dark auburn locks covering her face from view as she studied, and she was completely oblivious to the world around her. He was used to seeing her like this. Whenever she found a book that interested her, nothing could get her attention until she was finished. This was something that had frustrated their parents and teachers past the point of rationality on several occasions, yet both were always

amazed when all he had to do was walk up to her and her
attention would instantly be on him.

Of course, nobody else had known about their special
way of communicating, so they had no idea that he was
actually sending her images meant to disrupt her
concentration. While she had always seemed to be the
stronger of the two, and could occasionally send him
images with sound, he could only manage enough to
distract her from what she was currently doing. She
joked that his 'sendings' were like the fly that bites
at the horse's ass. Try as she might to bat it away, it
kept coming back until she was forced to squash it.

His eyes squinted as he mustered all the
concentration he could to send her an image of himself
approaching. As always, it was just enough, causing her
to jerk back to reality. As always, she turned toward
him with a smile.

"Well, well. Glad to see you back in the land of the
living big brother! You know, most people undress
BEFORE they wash." She chuckled as she closed the book
in front of her.

"I haven't gotten that far yet," he offered poorly.
"What's that you're reading," he asked as he took a seat
next to her.

"It's the journal of our grandfather's father. I've
been looking at it all morning. It's actually very
captivating! I think it details the exact moment when
our family first came into contact with vampires!"

She spoke very excitedly, and the words tumbled from
her mouth in a rush of emotion. He couldn't help but
smile and, as he felt her excitement flowing out to him,
he soon found himself listening raptly as she described
all that she had read thus far. She had read everything
up to the point where their great-grandfather had walked
back to his laboratory, with holy water dripping from
the cuff of his sleeve and running down the back of his
fingers.

"So, you mean to tell me that the hammer that
grandfather showed us-"

"Exactly! It's the same one that he used to pound
the stake into the chest of the vampire!"

He leaned back on his stump as the information
continued to sink in and studied his sister for a few
seconds. When they had sat around The Round Table the
night prior, he hadn't been too sure how to take the
information that was being imparted to them. He'd felt
guarded and had been waiting for Aedesius to suddenly
burst into laughter. But that hadn't happened and today
Jessie was really eating it up.

"What a minute, brother. I know that look you're
getting. You're thinking that this is just too much,
aren't you."

He twitched from the shock of being caught and it was
a moment before he could find an answer.

"I can't hide anything from you, can I sis," he asked
with a chuckle. "It's just that this IS a bit much.
Don't you think so? Before our parents died, I'd never
seen Aedesius before. And now here we are, entrusted to
the father of our father, living in the middle of forest
and training to take on the forces of evil. I just
don't know about all this yet. If vampires and
werewolves are real, why haven't we seen them before?"

She nodded as he spoke and when he was done, she laid
one of her hands over his arm before answering.

"You're right, as always. It does seem a bit
fantastic doesn't it? Do you think it's possible that
he's putting us over?"

"I don't know. Anything's possible when you consider
he's a man living in the middle of nowhere, I guess.
Where is he today, anyway?"

"He's hunting. He wanted me to remind you of the
meat that's still smoking out back and to tell you that
he wouldn't be back for a few days."

"Hunting" He trailed off as if to imply something
other than animal.

"He didn't say," she answered with a shrug. "Either
way, it occurs to me that we haven't really played since
we got here, and I don't know about you, but all this
work is lowering my spirits. What do you say I put this
stuff away and we play a game?"

She had a mischievous look on her face as she grabbed
the book and skipped back to the cabin. He already knew
what he wanted to play. There was still enough light

left in the day and there were literally a thousand
places to hide. By the time she had returned, he had
pulled a length of ribbon from one of his pockets and
tied his hair into a horse's knot.

"You STILL have that old thing," she asked in a
squeaking falsetto.

He smiled sadly before answering. "It's all I have
left of her." They both knew that the ribbon had been
around the last gift their mother had given them, just
as she knew he would likely carry it, or remnants of it
for the rest of his days.

"Constables and Criminals, that's what we're
playing."

"Oh, I'm the Criminal, I'm the Criminal. Catch me if
you can, you dirty copper!"

With that she darted away, squealing, and vanished
into the woods at the end of the property. With a sigh,
he followed.

From somewhere in the distance is a steady beeping.
While at this time of his life, he had no knowledge of
what an electronic noise was, something inside of him
identified it fairly quickly. He continued to run after
his sister, but as he approached the edge of the
property, the trees began to pull their roots from the
ground as they crept closer together. He tried to run
faster, to get there before they blocked off the
entrance to the wood, but it was too late.

"Jessie!"

It was no use. He called out to her, but he could
only hear her voice fading from behind the wooden
barrier.

"Jessie!!!"

"John?"

Her laughter had ceased, and when she called out to
him, he had thought that it was because she had heard
him. But the next sound only disproved that theory when
the silence was broken by her scream.

He banged his fists against the wall in front of him,
screaming for it to let him through, but there was no
answer. The light began to quickly fade, allowing
darkness to creep in around him, and his every instinct

97

warned him to get out of here this very moment. He
could not, however. His determination to protect his
sister forced him to stay. His confusion on how this
didn't seem right, how this couldn't have been the way
things happened, paralyzed him in his tracks. He was
conflicted, held by forces that he could not control and
when a dark figure began to material out of the
darkness, he felt an unfamiliar enemy creeping in.
Despair.

He turned to the right of the tree where moments ago
he pled to be let through. The darkness was
omnipresent. It wrapped it's tendrils around everything
it touched and it barely allowed enough light through
which he could see. Emerging from the depths was a
creature born of his worst fears. It slithered forward,
level with his eyes, but with a head that was wider than
his entire shoulder span. The speed at which it moved
boggled his mind, just as the image before him
threatened to tear a hole in his sanity, and it was only
seconds later when ten feet of black and crimson King
Snake, towered over him.

The creature was mostly the color of midnight, with
the exception of its belly scales, which were the color
of a pale eggshell. At the top of the serpentine tower,
the head of dark prince looked down at the young Van
Helsing with centuries of contempt. Its facial
structure was that of a human's, but the similarities
stopped there. The face was covered with scales. Where
a nose would have been were two large holes. The same
detail could also be said of the ears. It looked down
at him with evil red slits for eyes, framed by yellow
and full of all the evil of Hell. There was the sound
of a cloak being shaken and suddenly a cobra's hood
extended out to either side of the head.

It lowered its head, slowly, until one red slit was
just inches before him. The evil that radiated from it
was as foul as the stench that blew through its fanged
mouth every time it flickered out its tongue. From
somewhere in the darkness behind the creature, a steady
rattling continued to violate the silence that suddenly
surrounded them.

"At lassst we meet, Van Helsssing."

It was a young John Rizzerio that stood before the creature, but it was the mind of the man he would become that now inhabited this dream form.

"You! I'm going to-"

"What? Kill me?" The eye blinked before him, its inner lids appearing from the left and right sides of the eyes, and it seemed impossibly to smile.

"How do you propossse to do that, puny mortal? You can't even protect your friendsss when the time callsss upon you to!"

"…shut up…"

"I sssend my weakessst follower againssst you and the firssst thing you do isss get them all killed."

"Shut. Up!"

"Oh, come on John. Don't take it ssso perssssonally. Ssso what if you couldn't get the job done? Everybody fallsss every now and then."

The creature paused, punctuating its speech with the rattle of its tail, and it appeared to study him before continuing.

"There'sss nothing left for you, mortal. Your friendsss are dead, your family isss gone, and you no longer believe in yourssself to make a differenssse anyhow."

"ENOUGH!"

John lunged forward, leading with his right fist in an attack that was meant to blind, or at least stun, the creature in front of him. Mid-swing, however, he found that he was moving as if through water. Before he could even connect, the dark Prince snapped its head backward and whipped its tail forward in an attack of its own. As the segmented rattles of the tail came into view, John had only a second to react. His mouth fell open in surprise.

The tail arrowed forward and pierced the right side of his chest before pulling him into the air, back before the face of the vampire king. At that moment, its head seemed to waver in out and of reality until he was now looking at the human face of the Count himself. He wasn't handsome, nor was he ugly as well. His hair was pulled back in a warrior's knot, much like how John had secured his. It was as black as his scales, with

only the hint of white just above each of his ears. His
face is long, punctuated by a hawk-like nose, above
which are two glaring crimson eyes. There are some old
scars across the cheeks of his face, whitened by age,
that only just stand out on his milky skin, and he
speaks through lips that are the color of blood.

"I'm done with you, Van Helsing. Even as I speak,
you lie dying in two worlds. I'm disappointed. I had
thought that we would have a much grander battle than
'this'." He spits the final word out before flicking
J.R. from his tail, sending him spinning through the
air. John's flight is abruptly ended when he crashes
into the wall of wood, that was once the forest
entrance, and he tumbled the final four feet to the
ground.

The serpent lowers the illusion of its human face
before the gasping boy, chuckling softly.

"What could you posssibly hope to do againssst me?
You are but a child! You lack the POWER, let along the
EXPERIENSSSE to fassse the likesss of me!"

It lifted its head into the air, turning its body as
it slithered back into the darkness. With only its tail
still visible, John has just enough time to see, and
hear, its final rattle before he begins to slip into the
icy embrace of death.

As before, he can faintly hear the sound of something
beeping steadily in the distance. He tries to open his
eyes but is greeted only with confusion and blurry
images. His eyes close as he tumbles into the abyss.

IX

EXAMINING THE EVIDENCE

"It is with much chagrin that I inform you that you have been indefinitely suspended. At this time, I have to ask that you remove your badge and firearm and place them on the desk."

There was a pregnant pause as she waited for him to follow through with her request. Her heart was heavy as she watched one of her most dependable officers sullenly following an order she thought she would never have to give. He first removed his badge and slid it across to her. As he removed his firearm, she opened the top right drawer of her desk. Once both were before her, she slid them in and closed it before speaking once more.

"My hands are tied, Lachlan. This has been the hardest decision that I have ever made, and if I could find some way around it, I would. The fucker of it all is that the camera angle really makes it look like something took place between you and him. And, from where I stood, I'm not sure I could safely argue against that in court, if this were to go to trial."

He stood silently as she spoke, with shoulders slumped, and his eyes focused on the spot where he had moments ago lain the objects of his livelihood.

"Lachlan," she said softly. "Internal Affairs is breathing down my neck. Details have been leaked to the news about what happened at *The Clothing Store* and word is getting out about what happened in here as well."

"Who," he blurted more loudly than he had intended.

"I don't know yet, but believe me when I say that what you're getting right now is light compared to what's going to happen to the one who let this out. People are already talking about what happened in the containment area as well as in the interrogation room."

"I don't understand." But somewhere, a light clicked on in as he did indeed begin to do just that. And when she next spoke, it came as little surprise to him what she had to say.

"Jonesy. They're talking about how you were involved in both incidents. There have even been questions about what happened over on James Street."

Silence once again fell in the Captain's office as the gravity of her words began to set in.

"Niki, you know as well as I do how ridiculous this is! I was here when that shit went down! For Christ's sake, my blood runs blue for this department. Hell, for our city! No-one has ever been more dedicated to this job as I have!"

"But that's not how it looks from the outside!" Her voice noticeably changed, filling with frustration and anger that threatened to overcome her because of everything that had happened.

"They look at us and they see a man who either finishes or fills out reports to be filed by those who should be responsible for them. When they look in, they see a man who has unrestricted access to the evidence room. They see that I allowed this to happen, and damn it Lachlan, my ass is on the line here as well!"

"I'm sorry, I, uh, I didn't think of that way."

She looks across at him sadly as she considers his apology.

"I'm sorry too. I just wish there was some other way."

"It's alright Niki, I get it. I'll just get some of my things and clear out until this is over?"

She cocked an eyebrow, curious as to why he would have formed his statement into a question.

"You know, if there's anything the department can do for you…"

"You'll be the first to know."

He took a deep breath and offered her the most convincing smile he could muster. It must have looked convincing, she returned it in kind. As he turned to leave, she gave him the one last piece of advice which normally concludes these types of meetings.

"I know that you're already aware of this, but until the investigation is over, please try to stay in town."

"Yes ma'am," he answered as he left the room.

The office had been abuzz with chatter before he entered. Contractors were in the finishing the repairs

to the door leading to the containment cells. A slight
upgrade had been made, and once they were finished, a
security company would be installing a new touchpad door
system.

At the reception desk, a phone continued to hum
unanswered as the desk cop helped someone a few feet
away. Several other officers, including the one who had
shot the man who had confessed his name as Van Helsing,
were engaged in idle discussion. The interrogation room
had already been processed, and for the second time
today, the A.S.P.D. found itself fighting for some form
of normalcy.

As he stepped into the main office area, and with the
exception of the contractors and the phone, the office
instantly fell silent. All eyes turned to the senior
officer quickly becoming infamous for having some form
of involvement with the one that recently left via
coroner.

"All right, get back to work," yelled a voice from
behind him. Some of the men dispersed, returning to
their desks or offices, but a small few remained. Not
surprisingly, the cop who had pulled the trigger in the
interrogation room stood before the others.

"With all due respect, Captain, why isn't he going
down below?"

"With all due respect, Officer Melbourne, you're
talking about a man who has finished your reports on
more than one occasion. Also, if memory serves me, he
also filled in for you last month when your wife was in
the hospital?"

Melbourne's bravado faltered as he realized that she
had him. There was no denying her words; he had used
Jonesy's dedication to the squad many times over the
years.

"Yes ma'am, I guess he did."

"Then I don't need to repeat my previous order, do
I?"

"No ma'am," he answered grudgingly. The seed of
mistrust had already been sown in his eyes, and before
he returned to his desk, he made sure that Jonesy knew
this as well. As he turned, the few that remained with
him slowly returned to their desks.

Standing just behind him, Haubbes reached forward and placed her right hand on the side of his right arm in a silent show of support. He turned and smiled thankfully before returning to his desk to gather his things.

Twenty minutes later, he stood by the driver's side door of his Ford F-250 holding a large box he had found in the supply room. Inside were his personal possessions; inspirational pictures, a Newton's Cradle, several notebooks he used to keep track of everything he did, and an endless supply of desk supplies he had brought for his personal use.

These were all things important to him, but it wasn't these things which took up the majority of space in the large box. Carefully wrapped in bubble wrap, which he had conveniently borrowed from the supply room, were all of the items he had earlier stashed in the bottom drawer of his desk. His heart was racing as he set it in the bed behind the driver's side window and covered it with a small tarp he normally used to cover groceries.

"What's in the box, Jonesy?"

It took every ounce of willpower to not jump out of his skin when the voice spoke from just behind him. He knew, without turning around, that it belonged to the very same antagonist who had taken a stand against him a half an hour earlier.

"You were there when I cleaned out my desk, Sean, what do you think?"

"You know as well as I do that I had to take a call. What else you got in there besides those stupid books of yours."

He moved as if to reach into the bed of the truck but Jonesy stepped between the box and Melbourne.

"I don't believe there's any reason for you to conduct a search of my possessions, Officer Melbourne? Everything in my truck BELONGS to ME. There's no reason for you to have probable cause, nor will the Captain approve a warrant request for you to search my vehicle. Now, unless you want to make an ass of yourself, I suggest you get back to work son."

Melbourne backed a couple of steps away as Jonesy opened the driver's side door, climbed in and slammed it behind him.

"This isn't over, old man. There's something going on here and when I find out what it is."

"Yeah, yeah. You'll personally hold me responsible? Fuck off, shithole."

"You son of a-"

The rest of his curse was drowned out when Jonesy started his truck and revved the engine a couple of times before driving away. His heart thudded in his chest, beating a nervous tune he could feel in the tips of his fingers, the base of his neck, and just under his temples.

He drove a few miles to be confident that he hadn't been followed, before finding a place to pull over and regain his composure. He parked in the empty end of a Super-Center parking lot, just a few spaces in and facing the entrance. His hands started shaking, and he dropped his face into them when the enormity of his day suddenly caught up with him.

He felt like it might have been a waste of time, but he'd needed a good cry after everything that had happened to him today. If it had been any other day, he would have thought that he was going crazy. It any other person had revealed what John had, he would have had him committed. He tried to make sense of what had transpired back in that room. When John had touched him, there had been some form of transference that had taken place. He couldn't fathom it, let alone did he think he could ever explain it, but it HAD happened. That much he couldn't deny.

It wouldn't take long for the department to figure out that he had stolen the evidence. More critically, evidence that was directly linked to the case! Before he left, he had also packed up an evidence box, labeled it and had it prepared to be sent out to storage with the next pickup. At best, this would mean it had to sit for several hours before it was collected. It was a simple ruse, a good ruse if it worked, but it one that could easily be discovered as well. With Melbourne on his ass, this could be sooner than later.

Once this happened, he could consider his suspension permanent. More than likely, he would also be labeled as a person of interest with an A.P.B. put out on him as well! More than anything, he would have to act without any hesitation from here on out.

He dug into his pants pocket, grabbing his cell phone, and before he had it halfway to his head, he had dialed the numbers to the man he had contacted earlier about the translations.

"Yeah?"

"It's Jonesy. Remember those translations I needed?"

"Oh yeah, sure I do. Had to be the first time I ever heard of this language being used in these parts, but yeah. Say, what happened to you Jonesy? I thought you needed those scripts ASAP?"

"Something… Well, you might say that something came up. Actually, I have something that might be a little more interesting than those recordings I sent ya. Can you meet me at the 'net Café on Eighth and Morgan in an hour?"

"Sure. No problem. Say, you're not gonna be in uniform are ya?"

"…no," he said with a touch of remorse. "You might say that those days are falling behind me."

"Reeeally. Say, you wouldn't be interested in-"

"Nope."

He shut the cell phone off and tossed it into the passenger seat.

"What the hell does it matter if I'm in uniform or not," he asked angrily. It's not like they were going to be meeting at a place known for its questionable clientele. The 'net Café hosted many different types of people, from every rung of the social ladder, and it wasn't uncommon to see a man in a business suit seated next to someone who might be wearing an outfit that had just come from Good Will.

He was only a few minutes away from their meeting location, which gave him plenty of time to get familiar with the items in the back of his truck. Taking a last look around to make sure he was in the clear, he opened the door and got out. An occasional car pulled into the entrance, but there was nothing unusual enough about any of them to give him any alarm. As he reached in to uncover the box, he watched several people coming and going from the Super-Center's entrance. With the

106

exception of a small Asian man, most made their way to their respective vehicles at various points in the parking lot. The latter placed two bags in the rear basket of his bicycle and began pedaling toward the entrance.

As he was folding the tarp up and securing it, he heard his cell phone ringing from inside the truck. Grabbing the box, he climbed back in, set it on his lap and looked over at the phone's screen. It was Haubbes. Undoubtedly, the ruse had already been discovered. He sighed as he swiped the ignore option and then shut the ringer off. There was no sense in having it on at this point anyway, all of his contacts wore badges and would either be of no help or looking for him.

He cracked the window before removing the lid from the box. He was going to be too absorbed to notice any approaching sounds very soon, and at least this way he stood a pretty good chance at hearing anything that might pose him a threat. With a last look around, he noted the Asian man was a quarter of the way through the parked cars and would pass by him on his way out; he opened the box and reached inside.

He carefully removed his things and placed them on the seat next to him. First was his stack of notebooks. They were bound together with a rubber band and he easily sat them off to the side. He then removed several small Tupperware containers, inside of which were pens, pencils and various other supplies he had found himself needing over the years. These he sat aside as well. Finally, he removed his Newton's cradle, placed it on the dash and set it in motion. The steady clack-clack-clack brought a smile to his face, and he watched it in motion for a moment before turning his attention back to the bubble wrap at the bottom of the box.

As he reached inside, he began to feel a large amount of trepidation with what he was about to do. It wasn't too late for him make sure these things were processed. At least, after a brief glance at his phone, he didn't think so. He could simply return to the station and explain the mix-up, citing that the other box had his things in it.

He looked at the scar on his hand and shook his head. The moment for doubt had already come and gone a long time ago. He had made his decision when he walked through the entrance to the station with this box in his hands.

He let out a large sigh.

"Well, shit on toast. Here we go."

He had carefully wrapped each item in bubble wrap and he had to take them out one at a time. The bigger items he placed on the console between seats, while the smaller of the bundles he left inside of the box. Those smaller items were the ones he didn't need to look at in very much detail. They were just a few small vials, some ammunition and the man's cell phone. As he moved the box over to the passenger seat, careful not to spill his things when he set it down on them, the urge to take out the phone came over him.

"Might not be a bad idea," he thought to himself. His phone was compromised and this might buy him some time before he could get himself something more disposable. He leaned over and grabbed the phone, removed it from the bubble wrap, and quickly shoved it into the closest pocket.

He then focused his attention to the items left on the console. There were the man's weapons; a .357 Colt Python with the word Jessie scrawled in cursive on the barrel, a small hand crossbow, an old wooden mallet, and the curved dagger with a bell shaped hand guard. He was very careful with the last, having already discovered it to be sharper than any blade he has ever encountered.

Next to be unwrapped were a small bundle of books. One, which he had carefully rewrapped using the ribbon and cloth already around it, was a bible of which the material appeared much older than he. The same could be said of the other books as well. They were leather-bound and carefully tied closed to keep the papers from falling out.

Finally, he carefully unwrapped the final item he had lain out; the cross. He held it reverently, marveling at the craftsmanship, and was careful to not hold it over anything he didn't want to become stained. The Christ's back was arched away from the wood and he

108

looked heavenward as if pleading for mercy. Blood
trickled from its wrists and feet continuously, and if
left alone, he was sure that a sizable mess would
accrue.

The wood is rough in his hands. He doesn't feel
worried about getting a splinter; he knows the feeling
well enough to know that it was hand carved with care.
The body of the Christ is very detailed as well, more so
than any he has ever seen on a cross, and if he stared
long enough he could even make out every wound that the
son of God must have suffered before and after his
death.

There is a loud rapping sound on the glass to his
left and he jumps, surprised.

The Asian man is looking in, still seated on his
bike, with a blank stare on his face.

"Wha-?! Can I help you?"

His heart is pounding in his chest and he reaches for
the only weapon close enough; the Colt revolver.

"There is still time," the man answers cryptically.

"Time for, what, exactly?"

"You must go and wake the Mongoose before it is too
late."

A nervous chuckle bursts from deep down and it is
several seconds before he can muster his incredulous
response.

"The what?!" he laughs. "The Mongoose? What the
hell does THAT mean?"

The Asian doesn't answer and he doesn't get a chance
to think about it. At that moment, he feels something
moving in his hands and turns his attention away from
the cyclist to investigate.

Though nailed to the cross, the body of the Christ
has suddenly become active.

"Jesus, Mary and Joseph," he mutters breathlessly.

The Christ's eyes have opened and stare at him with a
look of misery unlike any he has ever known. It writhes
on the cross; arching its back as it struggles to move
away from wood that has now grown hot to the touch.

"Oh my dear Lord," he cries in dismay. "What must I
do?"

"You must help 'him'," the cyclist answers softly.

109

The man appears to first be looking at the cross that he's holding, but Jonesy sees that he is looking at the one book he had yet to inspect. Like the others, the cover is frayed around the edges. However, unlike those which where bundled together, the pages inside are still intact. Carefully written at the top were the letters; J.R.v.H.

"But, he's-" He had started to argue with what the Asian man had told him, but when he looked up, the man was gone. He looked at the entrance and as far as he could see either direction, but there was no sign of him anywhere. It was as if he was never there.

When he looked at the cross, the Christ appeared to be nothing more than marble once again. While it still trickled blood from its wounds, it no longer struggled to move away from wood now cool against his skin.

"What does this all mean," he asked silently. "Wake the Mongoose?"

He looked at the time and cursed, he needed to hurry if he was going to make his appointment. Jonesy took one last look at the items as he placed them carefully back into the box, and then set it on the floor in front of the passenger seat. He could only hope that his contact would be able to shed some light on the subject.

The 'net Café was fairly active for this time of day. He drove around the block twice before he found a spot close enough to park. Only thirty feet away, he was able to not only see the outside seating, but he would be able to see his truck from there as well. So, with little else to worry about, under the circumstances, he reached over and grabbed two objects from the passenger seat as he got out of the truck.

His contact was seated at one of the small tables outside. He wasn't hard to miss, not many people would have. He was well into his silver years. His hair had long since fallen out. His head was smooth and glared from the light of the sun. A small pair of reading glasses sat on the end of a large bulbous nose, the most dominant feature of a small face that showed his distinguished age. Many wrinkles defined his life, set deeply into his skin from many years of smiling. His hands were remarkably smooth, but this wasn't the detail

110

that helped him stand out in a crowd. He was fully
clothed in black, and just below his chin was the small
white square that identified him as a priest.

"Hello Father. I'm so glad that you could make it,"
Jonesy said when he came within range. The little man
stood with a smile on his face and his right hand
extended.

"Don't you think we're well past titles, Lachlan?"

"Sorry," he answered as he took his hand in greeting.
"I guess old habits die hard."

"So tell me. What is it that's got you all fired up.
First you want me to translate… Say, what has happened
to your hand?"

He reached up with his left hand and, still holding
Jonesy's left firmly in his right, turned it over to get
a better look. He sucked in a deep breath and it felt
like a lot of time passed before he next spoke.

"Where did you get that?"

Jonesy pulled his hand away and gently led the
smaller man back to the table where he had been sitting.

"I'll get to that, but first I need to show you
something. I need you to tell me what this is."

They sat, not at the table which Jonesy had first
seen him, but at a small table farther away from the
influx of customers. He reached into his jacket,
glanced around to make sure that they were not being
watched, and removed the Cross that had belonged to J.R.

As soon as it came into view, the priest reacted.
With a gasp, he lunged forward and placed his hand over
Jonesy's, motioning for him to replace it.

"You mustn't allow that to be seen," he whispered
harshly. "Put it away, lest the wrong set of eyes fall
upon it!"

Jonesy quickly replaced the Cross inside of his
jacket while giving him a funny look. If he didn't know
better, he'd say that the man had recognized it.

"What is it, Ezra? I mean; I know what it is, but
what IS it about this thing that's got you so spooked."

"Are you parked nearby," he asked. Jonesy was
suddenly afraid, based on the expression that had come
over the face of the smaller man, and he glanced around
nervously before answering.

111

"Y-yes. Just right over there, why?"

"Take me back to the church. It's safer for us to talk there."

Moments later, with Father Ezra in the passenger seat and the box securely resting in his lap, they merged into traffic and began the ten minute trip to where the priest held his congregation.

Jonesy reached into his jacket, removing the second of the two items he wanted to show him, and set it on the console between them. He passenger, however, waited several moments before taking it. He had grown pale and his hands, which had been laced together on top of the box, were noticeably shaking.

He carefully removed the ribbon from the bundle and unfolded the black cloth from around it. As he had when he had seen the cross, he gasped.

"Heavenly Father save us all;" were the words that quickly followed.

Nothing more was said between the two during the remainder of the ride. After seeing the bible, the elderly priest gingerly rewrapped it to its previous state and placed it in the box. Before closing the lid, he had peered in at the remaining items and Jonesy was deeply disturbed when he saw tears in the corners of the man's eyes.

Because the radio was rarely ever used in his truck, the only sounds in the cab were from the outside, or the occasional popping of the bubble wrap from the floorboards as his passenger adjusted his feet. Next to him, Ezra now held onto his rosary. And, while he could hear no sound from him, it appeared that he was praying upon each of the beads as well.

When at last the steeple to the church came into view, Ezra motioned for him to go around to a private entrance which was mainly used by the clergy. There was only parking for one vehicle, but there was also a bicycle rack for the more health conscious of people. There were two people seated behind the latter with their knees drawn to their chests.

"Is that normal," Jonesy asked when he saw them.

"Yes, yes," he answered in an off-handed way. "The church helps those who are less fortunate and takes care of those who have no fortuity whatsoever."

He nodded at the explanation, but felt extremely uneasy for some reason. His every instinct told him something was not right. The two had yet to move, even as the pickup parked just a few feet from where they sat. They appeared to be wearing long black trench coats over similarly shaded hoodies. The latter was pulled over their heads and dark sunglasses could just be seen covering their eyes. They wore dark gloves and jeans as well, all effectively covering every part of their bodies, with the exception of what little showed on their faces. Even then, these were hidden in the shadows beneath their hoods.

Jonesy looked over to his passenger, trying to determine if he wasn't the only one feeling uneasy, but he found no help in the other's expression. Ezra seemed to be lost in thought; his hands were still running over the beads of his rosary. He had just enough time to reflect on how slow things seemed to be taking place when the two men began to rise to their feet.

"Stay here," he ordered as he opened the door and stepped out. The eerie sense of time slowing down held nothing to the sense of danger in the air around him. His gut churned, tightening inside of him as he realized that he no longer had a gun. Furthermore, having changed into his civilian clothes before leaving the station, there was nothing about him to even suggest any authority should he need to use it.

He closed the door just as the two men began to approach. His expression became one of disgust when he noticed that there was something horribly wrong about their faces. From what little he could see, there appeared to be light green plating covering the skin, and if he didn't know any better, he would have sworn that they were scales.

"We're here for the priessst," the one on the right suddenly hissed.

"Give him to usss," the one on the left spoke shortly after.

"You can just stay right there," Jonesy warned. "What do you want with him?"

The two turned toward one another, both sharing a confused look before returning their attention to the former officer.

"It isss of no consssern to you," came the response from the man on the right.

From inside the truck, he could hear the sound of rhythmic chanting as it began to steadily increase in volume. He felt angry when, after everything he had been through today, he realized that he was standing outside of a church being threatened by these two goons.

"It is of every concern to me, sir, and I will advise you two just this once; leave peacefully and nothing more will come of this."

"Thisss isss your lasssst warning, mortal. Ssstep assside, and we will let you live," spoke the man on the left.

"*Mortal? What the fuck*," Jonesy thought to himself. At that moment, however, the two split away from one another. The man on the right moved as if to go to the passenger side while the one on the left began moving directly toward him. His nerves were put on edge as he realized that there was no getting out of this without conflict.

While both men were half his age, there seemed to be something wrong with each of them, and he had no way to defend himself should they have any weapons. As each continued on their course of action, a strange feeling began to come over him. His vision took on an unusual clarity, allowing him to see everything around him with as much detail as it would from a still shot.

Ezra was deep in prayer and the rhythm of his words affected him even outside of the vehicle. His words had become garbled, and yet, somehow familiar. He felt a strange sensation beginning to grow in his left arm, a tingling as if a thousand ants were marching circles around it from shoulder to wrist.

The scaly-faced goon in front of him took another step forward and had begun raising his arms threateningly. With no small amount of horror did he realize that the man's hands were covered with the same

114

kind of greenish scales that he saw on his face. The fingernails on each hand were also long and filed down to points.

His left arm began to rise on its own accord, moving into a position it had been in thousands of times over the course of his career. He was reminded of the feeling that he got when his arms floated to the top of the water while in the bath, and when his arm was fully outstretched before him, his palm facing outward in the universal gesture meaning "stop", he felt the tingling suddenly grow in intensity.

It was at that moment that time came rushing back to normal, and for the rest of his years he would question the events which happened next.

Out of the corner of his right eye he saw Ezra lock the doors and press his crucifix against the glass of his door window. He continued to recite the prayers associated to the beads, but he was no longer touching each one as he did so.

At that exact same moment, there was an intense itching sensation in the center of his left palm.

"I'm telling you now to turn away from here and leave us be," he yelled with much more force than he had originally intended. It had only been meant as a warning, but came out as the first phase in a multilayered spiritual attack.

"…AND DELIVER US FROM EVIL," were the words that Ezra suddenly erupted. The tingling sensation funneled down his arm, rushing with the force of an ocean current. The itching in his hand became unbearable, and his other arm jerked instinctively when the urge to scratch it compelled it to do what he had done all his life when he needed to relieve this very type of discomfort.

The other man had made it to the passenger side door, while the one in front of him was now a mere foot away. He saw its mouth beginning to open, impossibly wide, to make room for fangs that were pushing out from its upper and lower gums.

Suddenly, there was a tremendous amount of heat from the skin of his left palm and he started to look towards it with wonder as a bright light formed around it. There was no longer any time to react, for the light

115

then focused and took on the shape of the scar in his hand. A golden light, in the shape of a cross, shot from his hand and into the serpentine face of the man-shaped creature before him.

There was a sizzling, not unlike the sound of bacon frying, followed by an inhuman shriek of pain. The man, if it could have ever been called that, turned and leapt high into the air. Its movement was impossibly fast, however, and he didn't have time to watch its ascent as he turned the beam into the driver's side window.

The second creature had only moments before leaned toward the window, and was now grinning evilly at the old priest. Its mouth was opening in the same manner as the first and it displayed the same kind of retracting canines. The golden beam passed through the two windows, with the center of the cross aiming directly in the creature's mouth. There was a split second for them to register the expression of pain and surprise before it too, turned and launched itself into the air.

Jonesy followed this one's ascent, watching as it flew twenty feet through the air and onto a small office building across from the church. Later, nightmares of the creature scurrying up and around the side of the building would haunt him for many weeks to come.

Then, just like that, there was silence. The tingling sensation was gone with the golden beam of light, leaving behind a euphoric sense of peace.

X

WITHOUT LOOKING BACK

"Come inside. Quickly my son! It'll be safer in here than out there."

Lachlan stood with his mouth agape. So much had happened in the last few hours that he had not been able to reflect upon the entirety of it all. From the containment cells, to the interview room, and now this; there was no easy way to go about facing the reality of it. He was in shock.

The smaller man took him by his right elbow and with a furtive glace to where the creature had fled, proceeded to guide him to the church entrance. It took only a moment for him to find the key to the door and soon they were in a small room on the other side.

"You know?" Jonesy softly asked.

Ezra only nodded. His face was pale and his breath sounded labored. His crucifix dangled temporarily forgotten in his hand as he leaned with his back against the door.

"For how long?"

"Longer than you could possibly imagine. Come. Let us go where we can talk."

The priest had begun to walk into the Nave when Jonesy suddenly turned back to the door.

"Wait! The box!"

Before the smaller man could react, Jonesy slid the speakeasy open and peeked outside. It was quiet. The shadows stretched ever closer, looming over the narrow street between the church and the office building. Visibility was only about forty-five degrees in either direction, but it was just enough to see the box sitting on the hood of the truck.

"Shit," he muttered softly, followed by a hasty apology. He turned to where Ezra had last stood, an apologetic look on his face, but the priest was nowhere to be seen. "I've come too far to just lose the damn thing."

Without a moment's hesitation, he unbolted the door and stepped outside. The silence was eerie, not a single sound could be heard. There were no birds

chirruping. No traffic, human or otherwise, disturbed
the area for as far as he could see. The door slowly
creaked behind him and the hairs on the back of his neck
stood on end. He felt the presence of someone standing
very close and it took all of his willpower to not
charge out into the open.

"They're watching," whispered a soft voice from
behind him.

His imagination spun into overdrive. In the shadows
near the tail-bed, he could see thousands of shadowy
spiders crawling towards him. Near the street, a lemur
crouched ready to pounce. His eyes darted madly from
one place to the next, seeing dangers which weren't
there as his heart pounded deep inside of his chest.

"The Dragon has Come!"

*He suddenly recalled the words he had spoken earlier
this morning with crystal clarity. He could see the
pallid face of the Count looking down upon him. His
bloodshot eyes looked upon him with indifference,
holding no concern for the mortal who was pointing a gun
at him.*

*He could hear John chanting in his strange tongue
from somewhere downstairs, but the words were distant
and didn't make any sense.*

*"Put down your weapon. Swear fealty to me, lawman,
and I shall allow you to live in my service."*

*Jonesy had been frozen with terror, unable to answer.
The Patron of Vampires didn't wait for a response as he
stepped further into the room, quickly closing the
distance between the two of them. His hands had begun
to shake, something they hadn't done since he was a
rookie, as he leveled the pistol at Vlad's chest.*

He had been about to speak when…

…he felt a hand gently take his left elbow from
behind.

"They're atop the building there. Do you see them?"

The memory was fresh in his mind as he turned toward
the priest. Ezra was holding a small vial, very much
like the ones that had been in John's possessions, with
his thumb over the opening. When Jonesy had completely
turned to face him, Ezra immediately shook the vial in
his direction, spraying him as he signed the cross.

118

"It isn't much, more like a deterrent to these kinds of vampire, but it should be enough. Quickly now," he urged.

Jonesy didn't think; he reacted. With his truck in sight, he lowered his head and launched himself into a full sprint to the box. He closed the distance in no time, but as he knelt down to pick it up, he saw movement. Recalling the priest's warning, his eyes darted upward in time to see one of the creatures sliding down the side of the building. Except, sliding wasn't exactly the right word for what it was doing, it was more of a slither. If he hadn't been for the impending sense of doom, he could have laughed at the absurdity of it.

Quicker than his eyes could follow, the creature's feet were underneath of its shoulders and planted against the building, propelling it directly at the truck. Not waiting to see where it would land, he turned, pushing himself into a stumbling run back to the safety of the church. Ezra frantically waved him in, looking from him to something just over his shoulder.

He struggled to regain his balance, but it was a losing battle. His stumbling gait found his head and shoulders leaning more and more over his feet, until at the last moment, he fell just before the open door. The box bounced from his hands, sliding in between the legs of the priest, and he had just enough time to be thankful for that when he was suddenly grabbed from behind.

"Lachlan! No!!"

The church door began to rapidly slide away as he was dragged back into the shadows covering the street. He knew with an overwhelming certainty that he was going to die, and it made him even more determined to not allow it to happen. He wasn't going down without a fight.

As the truck began to slide by, he hooked his hands around the tire, momentarily stopping his assailant. He looked down to see what had gotten ahold of him and for the first time, he looked upon the true face of the Childe de Dracul.

It was one of the men from before, only now the hood and sunglasses weren't masking him. Dark green scales covered the face of a creature that could have once been human, but had since evolved into the monstrosity now before him. There was a small rise where a nose might have been, with two small holes for nostrils. Similarly, it had no ears, or any other discernible means of hearing that he could tell. Finally, its eyes were yellow with dark black slits for pupils. As Jonesy watched, a slender forked tongue flickered from its mouth.

"You ssshould learn to mind your own busssinesss, pig."

"Go to hell," he replied.

His left hand let go of the tire as he swung it at the creature. There was a satisfying *thup* as his fist connected with the right side of its face. It was a move that he had done countless times over the years, and it was executed with as much style as he could manage from his position. The creature's head turned slightly to the side, following the path that his hand had traveled, but then immediately snapped back to its original position. Its mouth opened slightly as it hissed at the former policeman.

"You'll pay for th—"

Its threat was ended mid-sentence as a six inch crossbow bolt slammed between its eyes. The creature hissed once more, but this time the source was not its mouth. The skin around the bolt began to bubble, reacting in the same manner as Alka-Seltzer would after being dropped into a glass of water. The vampire released Jonesy's ankles and its hands started clawing frantically at its face.

He began to scoot backwards, partially dragging, partially crab-walking himself back to the safety behind the church door. As his feet were passing the front bumper of the truck, the vampire's head melted, pouring its reddish-black inchor onto the asphalt at his feet.

"Jesus," he muttered in disgust.

At that moment there was a tremendous impact on the hood of the truck. Jonesy looked over as the back of the pickup see-sawed up into the air from the force of the second vampire's landing.

"Diiiieeeee," the second creature hissed angrily.

Much like the vampire that had grabbed him, this one's hood and sunglasses were gone. Its scales had a similar green coloring, but the similarities ended there. Around the top of its eyes, leading down the side of its head and around to where its ears would have been was a slight ridge. The scales on this ridge were black and yellow at its highest point.

The creature's fangs were completely extended from its mouth, a mouth which was now opened three times wider than a possible to accommodate for the curved upper and lower canines that were jutting forth.

It leapt from the hood of the truck, which had caved in from the impact, and landed with its feet on either side of Jonesy's waist. It then lowered its head before the former lawman, turning to the side so that the slit pupil of its right eye was looking directly into his left.

"I will drink you dry," it breathed. Its breath stank of decay and he was reminded of the time a mouse had died behind his refrigerator.

"Somehow I doubt that," he answered defiantly. "The A.S.P.D. already beat you to it."

It looked past him to the side entrance of the church and its eyes widened almost comically as another *twang* from the crossbow fired from behind him. The bolt missed its mark this time, only grazing the creature's cheek, but the damage was done. A large gash split it open just to right of its left nostril, circled around its cheek, and ended near the back of its head.

It shrieked in pain and leapt high into the air, hurdling itself back into the growing shadows. Jonesy, wasting not another moment, turned and scrambled back into the church entrance. As he crossed the threshold, Ezra reached down, grabbed a handful of his shirt and yanked backwards, further increasing Jonesy's momentum so that he could quickly shut and re-bolt the door behind him.

The two slumped against their respective walls and shared the same terrified expression. Ezra was alarmingly pale, his shaking hands still clutching onto the small hand-crossbow now sitting in his lap. Jonesy struggled for breath, his eyes darting between that of

121

the priest's, and to the speakeasy still open above the other's head.

"Were you scratched or bitten," the older man finally asked.

"Scratched? I thought-"

"If you are wounded, the venom from their fangs can still turn you as easily as if you were bitten."

Jonesy frantically looked himself over, but he didn't find anything to suggest he would be in danger of that happening. When he looked up from his self inspection, he noticed that the other was still pale and trembling, frantically struggling to retrieve something from his pocket but wasn't having any luck.

The younger of the two had seen something like this before, and after hurrying over to the older man's side, he reached into his pocket and removed a small prescription bottle. Quickly popping off the cap, he shook a couple small round pills into the priest's hand and helped steady it as the latter put them into his mouth.

Jonesy replaced the lid and set the bottle down between them, watching as the priest chewed the pills. A few moments passed before the color returned to Ezra's cheeks, and only when he was finally able to stop trembling did he speak.

"Let's gather John's things and go inside. We have much to discuss," he said weakly.

Jonesy silently obeyed and followed him through the Nave as the priest led him back into the Sanctuary of the church.

"Please wait here while I get us a drink," Ezra said softly, motioning toward a row of chairs used by the priest during readings.

Lachlan set the box down and waited, watching as the older man entered a door leading off the back of the platform. A few minutes later he returned with a small tray, on which were some crackers, two shot glasses, and a small bottle of bourbon. The old cop cocked an eyebrow upon seeing the last item, but the older man only shrugged off his unasked question, placed the tray on a seat between them and paused only to pour them each a drink.

They both gulped their shots, the older man with a slight grimace, and there was a moment where they each silently looked upon the large cross hanging over the altar.

"I think I need to know," Jonesy finally said, "everything."

The old priest only nodded as he chewed on one of the crackers.

"Starting with; how long have you been taking medication? And, are you okay?"

"Yes, I think so," he said. Some of the color had returned to his cheeks and he no longer trembled as he had before. "It's something that I've dealt with for a few years now. Doctor says I should lay off the drink, but you know how it goes."

Jonesy nodded solemnly. His attention was on the box sitting at their feet. He could see the brim of John's hat sticking up from beneath the books and he felt his resolve breaking. As the tears welled up inside of him, the second time today for a man he knew nothing about, Ezra placed a hand over his arm.

"Is he…?"

"Yes," he whispered.

"Then all is lost," the older man answered with a note of finality. "All we can hope to do now is to hold out for as long as we possibly can."

Jonesy lowered his head into his left hand, where his thumb and middle finger began massaging his eyes, and it was several moments before he spoke.

"How is it that you know him?"

The priest lifted his hand, leaned forward and reached into the box. After a moment of rummaging, he removed the book wrapped in black cloth.

"We met several years ago, when I was but a young man myself…

What will we do, John? We have nobody to turn to?"

The siblings stood before the funeral pyre, inside of which was the body of their grandfather. It had been built over 'The Round Table', where they had first learned of their destiny, and where they had later coordinated attacks against the various evil creatures that had surfaced.

"I don't know, Jess. I suppose we must make our way to the coast."

"Why there? Why not go to the city?"

The fire crackled as it hungrily consumed the wood and flesh it had been given. For several minutes this was the only sound. She studied his face, trying to get some idea of what he was thinking, but it had grown tight and emotionless since having found their grandfather the night before.

"He once mentioned the name of someone he trusted. We must go to see him."

The stood there until the fire had burned down to coals before grabbing their bags.

"Have you packed enough food?"

He already knew the answer to the question, but he wanted to talk about something to get his mind off of the past few hours.

"If you already knew the answer John, why did you even ask?"

"I'm sorry, it's just that-"

Jess wrapped an arm around his waist and laid her head on his shoulder before answering.

"Yeah, me too."

They stood this way for a few moments more before they slung their bags over their shoulders, and turned to look at the cabin one last time.

"Do you think we'll ever return?"

"No. There's nothing here for us to return to."

He reached down, grabbed an unburnt end of log and tossed the makeshift torch through the front window. The effect couldn't have been more dramatic. A low *fwoosh* preceded a wall of flames which quickly filled the interior of the cabin.

"What happened to their grandfather," Jonesy asked, curious.

"He had fulfilled his purpose," the other answered vaguely.

"I'm confused. How does telling me this answer my question?"

"Every story has a beginning my son. To understand how I came to know him, you have to understand how he came to know me as well."

"His sister, what was her name? Jessie? We should probably give her a call shouldn't we?"

The old man shook his head sadly, from side to side.

"She's been gone now for twenty years."

Ezra poured them each another shot of bourbon, downing his quickly before continuing.

"There is a large amount of time that passes between the moment they leave to cabin and the moment they arrived here. Many things transpire in their young lives, mostly horrible things, and it would be many years before we would meet."

"I don't get it Ezra. Aren't you the one that John spoke of before they left?"

"I'm afraid that was before even MY time!" Ezra laughs softly. "No, by the time I was sent to service with the church, John and his sister were already here serving the Lord."

"But, how is that possible?"

Ezra looked down at the bible with a thoughtful expression on his face.

"He was fulfilling his purpose." While it was the same phrase he had used for John's grandfather, when he used it this time, it was with great sadness.

Three boys knelt in the Sanctuary of the church at the steps leading up to the altar, behind which a priest in white robes was preparing communion. Seated in the pews of the Nave, their families watched as the priest came around and offered the body and blood of Christ to each of them. Only after each had accepted that Christ was their only Lord and Savior did he welcome them as disciples to the church.

Jessie watched from the shadows of the balcony while John sat quietly off to the side.

"What are you thinking about," she finally asked.

His was a sigh of irritation before he answered.

"Can't you just 'look' and see for yourself?"

He was immediately sorry when he felt the effect that the sting of his words had on her.

"I'm sorry Jess," he whispered. She had turned away and was watching the ceremony continue below. The priest was singing, off-key, in Latin as he blessed the future priests.

"I can't remember what it was like," he finally answered.

It wasn't hard for her to 'see' what he meant, the image of the two of them with their parents projected with his words, filling her with the same sadness he carried on his shoulders.

She searched deep inside of herself for the memories he sought and was dismayed when she wasn't able to draw upon them as well.

"There has been too much evil, too much sadness since they died. I cannot remember the last time we were happy."

She couldn't refute his words. They were the truth. She only continued to watch the scene unfolding below.

"I can't believe that this is what our lives will always be, can you?"

She turned to face him, studying him as he watched the congregation.

"I honestly don't know what's in store for our future, John. Each day, while you are helping restore the church's exterior, I'm reading every book I can get my hands on. Every day is a blur and I don't have time to think about what's coming next. Do I picture a future where we aren't hunting monsters? Yes, but I also know that if we don't do it, who will, or CAN, for that matter?"

For the second time, he sighed at her words. She was right, of course, but the burden was more than he could have ever imagined.

At the altar below, the ceremony was coming to an end. The parents of the boys walked up to their respective children and were saying their goodbyes, giving them what little they could bring from what was now their former lives. The shortest of the three, a sickly looking youth with sandy blond hair and spectacles sitting on the end of his nose, was looking up to where they sat.

"Huh," John muttered. Jessie turned to look where her brother's attention was focused and saw the boy watching them over the shoulder of his weeping mother, the latter who was clutching tightly to him even as her husband tried to separate her from their son.

"Do you think he…"

"…sees us?" He finished. Yes, I believe he does.

"So you met them when you gave your life to the church then," Jonesy stated more than he asked.

"No, that day I only saw them. Or more specifically, I saw John's eyes watching me from the shadows. At the time, I had thought I was seeing a vision from God."

"What do you mean?"

"John's eyes have this unusual quality about them. When I happened to look into the balcony that day, all I saw were two golden crosses floating in the darkness."

Jonesy looked at the side entrance of the church where the speakeasy was still standing ajar, as he thought about what the old priest had shared with him. He thought about what John had shared with him as well. Not only had he revealed his identity to him, but he had passed on a little of something else as well.

"This connection that John and his sister had. Was it only limited to them?"

It was a moment before the priest answered. He appeared to be mulling the question over in his mind, and he was working on yet another shot of liquor.

"When she was alive, I never knew him to be able to use it any other way."

"But?"

"There was a moment when, during his marriage to a young woman named Emily, I felt his mind reach out to mine. I don't know if it was intentional, but I saw an image of a vampire wearing a gray suit. Why do you ask?"

Jonesy then explained what had happened during the interrogation. He didn't withhold any of the details as he described everything from the moment he first walked in, to the moment that John had been shot, and by the time he was finished the eyes of both men were sodden with tears.

127

"It was just the one shot? You're sure that—"

"Yes," Jonesy answered. "When the Captain checked for a pulse, she found none. He was pronounced dead by the coroner only a few minutes later."

"I see." The words were choked as the old priest fought to maintain control. "Do you think there is some way that we can see the body before your coroner completes his, duties?"

Jonesy starts at the question, his eyes wide with confusion.

"I— I suppose so. But, why?"

"John was always under the impression that he couldn't die unless there was an heir to succeed him."

"It might be too late," Jonesy conceded. "Are you thinking…?"

Since his third shot, the priest had begun to regain some of the color to his cheeks. Placing the bible back in the box, he grabbed the tray and slowly stood, looking down at the former cop with something that was as close to hopeful as he could manage.

"One can only pray."

Ezra walked to the back of the Sanctuary and entered the door from which he had retrieved the meager food and drink. There was the sound of a faucet running and of glasses clinking together from the next room as, Jonesy presumed, the older man cleaned the glasses they had just used.

While he waited, he reached into the box and removed the revolver. The detail put into the scribing of the name was very detailed. The script was clean, without any visible starting or stopping point between letters, and he would have been hard pressed to agree on whether it was done by hand or machine. He opened the chamber, which revealed to him that it was fully loaded, and removed one of the bullets.

"Amazing," he uttered breathlessly. Much like the bell guard over the handle of the dagger, the bullet was also intricately covered with holy markings and symbols.

When he heard the approaching footsteps of his companion, he loaded the bullet back into the chamber, snapped the barrel closed and laid the weapon across his lap. Ezra now wore a small satchel, much like the larger one rolled up in the duster at the bottom of the box.

The elderly priest knelt at the altar, making the sign of the cross, before standing and walking over to the pedestal which held the baptismal waters. As Jonesy silently watched, he removed several small vials, filling each of them before replacing them in the satchel.

"Lachlan," he said without turning to look at him. "Would you mind looking through the speakeasy?"

"Y-yes Father. But what am I looking for?"

Ezra smiled, using only the right side of his mouth, before answering.

"Everything. But, hope for nothing." He put the last of the vials into his satchel, which Jonesy mused resembled the one worn by a certain whip wielding archaeologist from the silver screen, and finally turned to face him. For the first time since meeting him this afternoon, Jonesy watched as the older man moved across the Sanctuary with the energy of a man half his age.

"Come now, hop to it."

Jonesy stood, grimacing when his back suddenly creaked in protest, but moved to the door as he had been asked to. It had become considerably darker outside. The shadows now covered everything between the church and office building, and the street lamps were beginning to hum as the lights inside of them flickered on.

His truck sat where he left it, though it was now a total loss. The center of the hood was folded in where the second vampire had landed, and the front axle underneath was broken. Where the first vampire had fallen was a reddish-black puddle of steaming liquid. A foul looking cloud hovered over the remains, and even from here could he smell its stench.

"The truck's no good. We're going to have to find some other way."

"Can you see anything else?"

"Nothing," he answered after scanning the edges of the building. "It's too dark to make out anything."

"Mmm… It looks like we're going to have to do this the hard way. Alright then, I want you to go to the back for me. In the room behind the door I entered earlier, and off to your right, is a staircase leading up. I want you to follow it up to the second floor. There you will find a hallway with several rooms on either side. Behind the only closed door, you will find a large backpack, the kind normally used for camping. Bring it here."

"Why do we need that?"

"Because," the priest said while motioning toward the box. "You're going to need your hands free."

Jonesy followed his directions and reached the room at the top of the stairs. True to the old man's word, the backpack was in a room behind a closed door. Upon entering the room, however, he found himself wishing there was more time to explore. The walls were covered with hand-drawn sketches, everything from human, to monster. Some he recognized, while others he had never even heard of.

When he returned, Ezra helped him load John's possessions into the backpack. The duster, they rolled up and stored underneath, with the hat fastened over it.

"Wear that," the priest spoke of the revolver. "We might have need of it."

"I thought you didn't condone violence," Jonesy asked.

"Only against one another. Those creatures," he said, motioning to the door, "they're not of 'His' design, and therefore, they don't count."

Jonesy strapped the .357 Jessie around his waist. He smiled as he briefly entertained ideas of how he felt like a gunslinger at that moment with the revolver at his side and its belt loaded full of bullets.

"I'm ready when you are," he said to the priest as he clasped the buckles of the hiker's backpack over his chest.

The old man sighed and looked back into the church for the last time.

"How far is it from here?"

"About an hour's walk, give or take; we should be fine as long as we keep moving. Are you sure you're up for this?"

Ezra nodded thoughtfully.

"He would do the same for us."

130

With that he opened the door and they stepped into the darkness beyond.

XI

BROKEN

He could hear the sound of something raining down on
the ground around him. It was an unusual sound, one he
didn't at first recognize, and when he pictured his hand
rummaging for a bite of popcorn he was immediately
confused. Popcorn? That didn't sound right, did it?
Had he fallen asleep while watching a movie? And two,
why the hell would it be raining popcorn?

He slowly opened his eyes, only to be greeted by an
image even more confusing than what he had just
imagined. The first thing he noticed was that
everything was blurry. He was looking to the left and
thought that he could see what might be a desk, but it
was too out of focus for him to tell.

There was a raspy creaking in front of him, prompting
him to turn his head and find the source of the curious
noise. As he looked at the boxlike object swaying over
him, his memories began pouring over the haze of
confusion.

He had escaped!

Each time the box swayed over him, some of the pine
shavings slid out and fell on or around him. When he
tried to roll to his right, he was immediately stopped
by a bright spark of pain unlike any he had ever felt
before. It began in the middle of his right arm, shot
up through his shoulder, and followed the nerve endings
to his brain, endlessly screaming its message of agony.
He cried out in pain and turned toward its source, only
to be baffled when he didn't at first see it. Where his
right arm should have been was nothing but empty space!

He screamed in terror as he suddenly recalled the
last image he had of his late friend, and rocked to the
left, clawing at the ground with his left hand. The
pain intensified and he felt himself beginning to lose
consciousness.

*"A-ten-hut soldier! Do you honestly think you have
time to take a nap? Get your scrawny ass up and moving
before someone discovers what happened!"*

The ghostly voice had traveled a long way before it
was able to reach the little man, but it was just

enough. His eyes snapped open and he struggled to pull himself up and into a sitting position. Never in his life had he ever felt anything like this, but it hurt even more to imagine the last few seconds that Brody had had to endure. Finally, he was sitting. Something heavy bumped into his right side and he cringed away from it, protecting his face with the back of his left arm. Only when nothing happened did he peek through tear-filled eyes to see what was pressing against him.

At first he was first elated. It had only been his right arm, which had been previously pinned behind him on the ground. The relief quickly passed when he saw the state that it was in. His arm was broken in two places, once just above the elbow and the other behind the wrist. It was bent in such a way as to suggest that his body had suddenly decided to form two new elbows, each bending in their own direction. The black discoloration around the wounds and the shooting pains told a different story. To top it off, his arm was out of its socket and hanging at his side.

His vision began to swim out of focus, but this time he gritted his teeth and fought against it. He recited passages from some of his favorite books, and only after several minutes was he able to regain control of his fading consciousness.

The pain still came and went in waves, but his mind was monotonously continuing to recall anything it could in order to distract him from it. He felt another moment of confusion as he looked around. It suddenly occurred to him the impossibility of what had happened in here while he was in the box.

John had been in, and escaped from here over twenty years ago. So how could he have seen the bodies still lying where his friend had described them? As he looked around he also noticed that, with the exception of the small break area, a thin layer of dust covered everything. There was a small tray sitting on one of the tables closest to where he had been suspended, on which was a plastic cup full of water and a couple slices of stale bread.

"You don't have time to worry about that right now!"

Though it still continued to sound as if spoken from over a great distance, it couldn't have had a more dramatic effect. He came back from his reflections with a start, followed by a small yelp, when the involuntary action sent another wave of pain up his right arm. Brody was right, of course. He could worry over the details later, after he was safely in the care of his ageless friend.

He leaned forward and placed his left hand on the floor, bracing himself as he tucked his feet under him. Once he was crouching, he stopped long enough to grab his phone, which he found just in front of him and beneath a small pile of shavings.

"J-just in c-case," he assured himself.

It was difficult work, and never in his life had he thought he would have as much trouble standing up, but he finally managed to get himself vertical with the aid of a nearby chair. His breath came in short gasps, and tears streamed from his eyes, as he tried to recall which direction led to the outside.

There were several tracks in the dust, around the break table, which led to and from the back of the warehouse, but this didn't seem like the smarter direction to travel. While it was closer to an exit in that direction, there was likely to be more guards there. Across from him and closer to a pile of rubble that was nearly as tall as he, was a path in which there were only one set of tracks. He tried to remember what he had seen in the moonlight, but now he wasn't so sure. Where the pile of broken boxes was, *might*' have been where the worker had been crushed...?

Tears rolled down his cheeks as a combination of pain and despair swept over him.

"Get a move on it, little buddy. There's... not... m..."

"Brody?"

When there was no response, he frantically looked around as he tried to decide what his next course of action might be.

"W-what am I s-supposed to do now," he cried in anguish.

His searching eyes finally came across something that held the answer, and even though he wasn't aware of it

134

at the time, it was this object that forced him into
action. Sliding his phone into his pants, he grabbed
the small notebook from the edge of the desk and began
making his way to the corridor behind the rubble.

Each step forward sent a river of fire coursing up
the nerve endings in his arm, and as he followed the
footsteps back into the corridor, he began to wonder
just how far he was going to get. When J.R. had
recounted his own harrowing escape from this place, he
had described an empty landscape just outside the door.
And while it was true that there were plenty of street
lamps for him to see by, this warehouse was set far from
any other building, with the nearest one being over two
miles away.

There was nothing left but for him to try. He passed
the broken crates and paused long enough to look down at
the footprints.

"So, t-that much is t-true," he muttered softly.

The prints were very human up to the point where he
was standing, where they then became very much canine in
shape and structure. He looked around for a moment,
trying to determine where they led from here, but he saw
nothing to support any evidence as to which direction
the tracks went. It was as if they just disappeared.
There was a dull pain beginning to form behind his
temples as he tried to make sense of everything, but it
was as if there was a dense patch of fog was covering
his memory.

From somewhere behind him, near the back of the
warehouse, he heard a reverberating *click*. His eyes
darted to the other side of the clearing, but when
nothing else followed, he slowly exhaled and entered the
first corridor.

The steel shelving stood several feet over his head.
They were packed with crates of varying size and color,
making it impossible to tell which direction he was
traveling. His only saving grace was his memory. When
John had escaped, he had done so through a rain of
bullets and debris.

He looked around and sure enough; there were still
signs of his friend's previous escape. While the crates
had long since been replaced or removed, he was able to

find markings in the steel from the bullets that struck them all those years ago.

He tried to imagine what it must have been like for John. His friend had blindly fled past row after row of crates, arms protectively covering his face from the raining debris. He thought to himself; *"If John had been able to do it, blind, there isn't any reason I shouldn't be able to do it with just one arm, right?"*

Seconds stretched into minutes as he plodded along. The work area, where he had been recently imprisoned, had long since slipped behind him, moving further away as he continued on to what he hoped was the exit.

click

His heart jumped into his throat. The sound was closer this time and he thought he heard a soft scraping follow shortly behind it. Again, he held his breath as he listened. With the exception of his eyes, he was perfectly still as he searched the corridor behind him. When he could hold his breath no longer, he slowly exhaled, but he remained watchful until his breathing returned to normal.

Panic was beginning to set in, he could feel it. He could feel the presence of another closing in on him, stalking him as he slowly made his way out of the warehouse. When he could stand it no longer, he turned and began to move as fast as he dared without causing himself further injury. He grabbed the sleeve over his right arm and pulled it close to his body, grimacing through the pain that it caused. As much as it hurt, however, he reminded himself that whatever they had planned on doing to him was going to hurt a whole helluva lot worse than this.

With a determined look in his eyes, he tucked his chin against his chest and ran with a loping gait, which was the best he could muster. The first few steps were the worst and twice his vision blurred from the pain, causing him to careen into the steel shelves and bounce off of the crates that were slightly hanging into the aisle.

Finally, after what felt like a nightmarish eternity, he burst free from the shelving and into a small waiting area. It wasn't exactly a room, in the same sense that the clearing hadn't been a room either, but it did have a separate feel to it. Ten feet in front of him was his exit. A large bar was securely placed over it, resting in 'J' shaped cradles that were bolted to the wall on either side of the door, thus securing it from outside entry. A small receptionist's desk was off to the right, thankfully unoccupied, while to the left were four folding chairs with a coffee table sitting before them.

"Damn," he muttered.

He carefully let go of the sleeve on his right arm as he entered the waiting area. A quick glance over his shoulder revealed three corridors, including the one he had emerged from, that converged at this point. For the moment, all three were empty.

"I d-don't remember J-john t-talking about th-this…"

As he slowly entered the room, he focused all of his attention to finding a way to get the door open. With one arm, the bar would be almost impossible for him to lift. Even if he'd had the use of both arms, he would have been hard pressed to get it out of the cradle. While the bar was only two by four inches, it was made of solid steel instead of wood.

"W-wait a m-minute," he said, following the bar to the right of the door. He had seen a mechanism like this once before and if he was right… The bar connected to an electronically controlled hinge! He just had to find the switch that controlled it!

Another bout of dizziness passed over him as he turned away from the door, briefly causing him to lose his balance. Luck is with him as the small desk is close enough for him to prevent himself from falling completely to the ground. While the pain had become a steady reminder that he was on borrowed time, his determination brought him once again back into focus.

He lurched, and for a moment he thought he was going to be sick, but the feeling slowly subsided. He didn't know how much longer he could hold out, but what he did know was that he had to get out of this hellish nightmare before he was discovered missing.

Walking around the desk, and using his good arm to steady himself, he began to search for the button that he knew would open the door. He checked above the keyboard slide-out, inside the top drawers, and beneath the armrests of the chair. Nothing. Frantically, he searched inside the bottom drawers. Still nothing.

He was looking up in frustration when he saw the small box attached to the wall. It was near the floor and behind where the receptionist sat. In this way, he or she could simply reach back, flip open the cover, and push the button to open the door!

Getting low enough was a challenge, but he managed to get into a crouch just long enough to press the button. It worked just like he thought it would; like a charm, and an electrical hum filled the room as the lock bar lifted out of its cradle and away from the door.

"What the fuck!? Who the hell's opening the door!?"

The voice was far enough away that he didn't have to fear getting caught before getting out, but it added an element of danger that he didn't really need right now. He wasn't John. His wounds wouldn't mend quicker than anyone else's, nor did he have the stamina that Brody had possessed. He didn't think he'd be able to make it to safety before they caught up with him, and that was assuming they didn't just shoot him in the back and be done with it.

The bar locked into an upright position and he wasted no time returning to the door. Acting on instinct alone, he threw it open and burst out into parking lot beyond.

As the door bounced shut behind him, and the lock bar automatically returned to its downward position, he instinctively looked over to his left, to the parking spot John had described himself arriving in all those years ago. It was empty, and except for the dark oil stain in the middle, one would have to wonder if it had ever been used at all. Weeds grew through the concrete in several places, where it had cracked from the heating and cooling that came from years of wear.

He stood there for a moment longer, shielding his eyes as they adjusted to the overwhelming brightness assaulting them, and he wondered how far he would be able to get before he either passed out or they caught up with him.

"W-we shall h-have to see," he said with resignation in his heart.

His escape was much different than J.R.'s. While John had been running with only superficial injuries, he was only able to run in such a way that reminded him of a certain hunchback from a black and white movie he had seen several years ago.

"And so our unlikely hero escaped from his prison. Having had no food or water for days, with his right arm broken and swelling with infection. How long would he be able to hold out against the odds?"

He chuckled at the narrator's voice. He wasn't sure if was a figment of his imagination or if he had actually heard it, and truth be told, he didn't really look too much into it. Delirium was beginning to set in. He had never been a strong runner and whenever he had been called upon to hurry; his best was almost always never good enough.

His arm had begun to swell, just as the phantom narrator had suggested, and the pain was becoming a manageable throb as it flopped randomly from the side of his stomach to the middle of his back. The ground rolled by beneath his feet, and he found himself giggling once more. This time because he pictured himself running on a treadmill on which the tread was made of freshly mown grass.

He could feel himself slipping away, like he had many times before since having tumbled from the box, and his legs wobbled unsteadily beneath him. Suddenly he was no longer going forward. No longer in control, he took three unsteady steps backward and fell into a sitting position with his legs splayed out in front of him. The last thing he saw, before the darkness rushed in to claim him, was the edge of highway just inches over the tips of his toes.

He had fallen asleep, in his favorite chair, in a position that he was very used to finding himself sitting in. He had been up late the night before, as he had on countless other nights, researching the paranormal. His head was slumped forward with his chin resting on his chest, when he had been awakened by an incessant ringing.

At first he was confused. For some reason he felt like he was in two different places at once, but that quickly passed as the urgency of the phone prompted him into action. He sat up and tried to reach for the receiver with his right hand, but it wouldn't respond. Had it fallen asleep? Possibly, but he didn't think about it for very long. He rose on wobbly legs and answered the phone with his left.

"Hey there, little buddy. You got a minute?"

At first he didn't answer. A feeling of déjà vu, so strong that it drove him back into his seat, had come over him.

"Quinn? Are you there? I need someone to talk to."

Of course the voice belonged to Brody, but he hadn't talked to him since the battle with Draegan (he died).

"Y-yeah, I'm h-here. It's j-just that w-we haven't heard f-from you in y-years!"

"I uh… I've been having a hard time Quinn. I don't know how to deal with this, you know? Listen, I really need to talk to you about some of this. I think I'm losing it!"

"Y-yeah, sure. A-anything!"

"It's just that, well, ever since that night I have been seeing these things everywhere. Shit man, I've even had to take a few of 'em down! I don't know what's real anymore."

His voice slurred as he spoke. The pain behind his words hurt him, just as much it must be hurting his bigger friend, and he sat quietly trying giving the man what he needed; someone to listen.

"Did you know that John and I served together?"

He did, but he answered anyhow.

"Y-yeah, I remember y-you telling m-me that once."

"Have I ever told you about the time I killed a kid?"

He didn't have time to answer, let alone swallow this horse sized pill of information, before Brody continued.

"We were stationed outside this shithole of a village. It was in the middle of nowhere, and we were only supposed to be there long enough to get our new

orders. Maybe a day, two at most. It was absolutely
beautiful there. You see, the village was at the base
of a mountain, from which tumbled the bluest waters I
have ever seen. There was this mist in the air. Maybe
it came from the waterfall, I don't know, but it hung
over the village the entire time we were there.

John and I had been on patrol, while the rest of our
squad remained at the base of operations. Now, can you
imagine how beautiful it was? All the greens, the
spraying mist, the warm air? It was heaven on earth my
friend, and nothing could ever ruin it. Or so I
thought.

We were bullshitting about everything and nothing,
anything to pass the time, when out of that mist comes
this little boy. I knew immediately that he was the
enemy. Sure, his clothes and slanted eyes gave him
away, but it also had more to do with the AK-47 he was
carrying.

He started waving the rifle at us and screaming. I
didn't know what the hell he was saying, but John sure
did. I could tell because this frightened look suddenly
came over his face. I didn't think Quinn, I reacted.
The boy was lowering the rifle at us when I drew my side
arm and, and…"

His friend burst into tears at the memory he was
reliving over the phone, and Quinn only listened
sympathetically. He listened, but his thoughts
continued to be distracted as he tried to regain some
feeling in his right arm. He was contemplating pinning
the receiver between the right side of his face and
shoulder, so that he can rub some feeling back into it,
when Brody finally calmed down enough to continue.

"I wouldn't wish this upon my worst enemy," he
started slowly. "I had thought that killing women was
bad enough. It couldn't be helped, you know? We were
just following our orders by taking out the targets, but
there was always a woman willing to pick up the target's
fallen weapon. That's just how strongly their beliefs
were! There hasn't been a day when I've wondered if it
was us who were truly the enemy in that war."

"I h-had no idea," Quinn murmured softly.

"No. No, I suppose you don't, do you?" He takes a deep breath and slowly exhales before he next speaks. "Listen to me, whining about something that can't be changed. You know what I mean? Humanity, it's something that we all have in common. It doesn't matter if we're white, black, red, yellow… We're all human!

That boy, he was willing to die for his people because he saw US as the enemy. That 'look' on John's face? The kid was telling him that we needed to go, that if we didn't, he would kill us. He was giving US the chance that, when the roles were reversed, we never even considered!

What person wouldn't do the same, given the conditions those people had been put in? If it had been me at that age and the soldiers were Russian? I would have done the same. Wouldn't you? I mean, I know you do your work in that little notebook of yours, but wouldn't you feel compelled to remove the enemy at whatever cost?"

Quinn thought about it for a minute before answering. "Y-yes, I t-think so-"

"Of course you would," he answered, elated that his friend agreed with him. "You're cut from the same mold as I am! You're just wearing a different skin."

This seemed to strike him as funny, but it only sent chills down Quinn's spine.

"You know? Since we rescued Emily from the bowels of that shithole, I have killed more monsters than I can count. Can you believe that? I have killed seventy-two people in my life; fifty one men, nineteen women and one child but I cannot, for the life of me, tell you how many of those goddamn things I have sent back to hell!"

"Hey! Hey buddy, are you… Oh my god. Marge, call 911!"

Someone was gently holding onto his right shoulder but when he tried to open his eyes, he couldn't make anything out. He saw everything through a veil of pain which was blurry and spiteful at the idea of him being awake.

"Bring me a bottle of water honey, qui…"

"I'm tired, you know? I just want to take all of my things and retreat to one of those underground bunkers they keep talking about on TV. No phones, no paper trails, nothing. I want to go somewhere where everything makes sense again."

He was only partially listening to his friend at this point. He suddenly wasn't feeling well, and for a moment he had been daydreaming that an elderly man was leaning over him. He felt a strong sense of disconnection within himself, pulling him in two different directions at once.

"You still there, Q-man?"

"Y-yeah, I'm h-here."

"I'm sorry to bother you so late at night, my friend. I just needed to get some things off my chest, you know? This whole business of being a vampire hunter, or monster hunter, or whatever the fuck you call this; it's just not for me. It's just too hard.

You wanna know something? When I was in the military, I promised myself that I would always remember the names of every person I've ever served with, but now? Now there is one name in particular that I'd like to forget."

Of course he knew who his friend was talking about. The last time they had gotten together was about a week after the battle with Draegan, and it had only been long enough for them to say their goodbyes. They had all agreed to split up for a while, with the exception of J.R. and Emily, and lay low until they could figure out what to do next. The latter two would stay near All Saints, where she could be close to her family. They had also chosen to remain behind in case anything should turn up with Jessie. Though he claimed to know that she was dead, they had found no trace of her having been in the building while they were there.

"Hey, I know that you are probably in the middle of one of your books or something… I have to go anyways, there's a bit of an undead problem down here and I should probably do something about it."

"Y-you weren't b-bothering me, old f-friend…"

"No, it's no big deal. Listen, it's really good to hear the sound of your voice Quinn. Even if I did just

143

*do most of the talking, I think I needed to have
something from the old days. I'll give you a call when
I'm done here. Maybe you can tell me what you've been
up to?"*

*He chuckled as he said goodbye and a few seconds
later he was listening to an empty dial-tone. It really
had been too long since they had talked and he was glad
that his friend had called, even if the news he was
sharing wasn't all that great. He carefully set the
receiver back in its cradle and turned his attention
back to his arm.*

"…no sir. The missus saw him just sitting there, and
the first thing we did was call 911."

"And there was nobody else nearby that you could see?
No vehicles?"

"Nope. Like I said, he was just sitting there. When
I first looked at him, I had thought he was…"

The voices became faded away, and this time when he
closed his eyes, there were no dreams.

Much like the first time, when she awakened, there was a steady electronic beeping just to her right. Every so often she would hear a machine humming, accompanied by the sound of crinkling paper. The room was dark, and if it wasn't for the beam of light shining in through the bottom of her door, she wouldn't have been able to see the rudimentary shapes around her.

There was a small table just to the right of where she lay. It was the kind that was built to roll under the bed, while the table itself floated over the patient, so that one would have a place to eat or to set their things. Atop the table is a vase filled with some kind of pleasant smelling flowers. She wished that she could see what kind they were, they had a wonderful scent!

The shadows were darker on the right and left side of her bed, making it difficult for her to see much else. She looked around through squinted eyes for several minutes, and at best she thought she could make out the shape of a couch off to her left.

Beyond the door, under which the light was shining, she could hear the murmur of several distinct voices. Just as she had tried to make out the shapes in her room, she turned her head from one direction to the other in an attempt to make out what the voices were saying.

"…*police department?*"

"*Yeah, from what I understand, they were interrogating him when he suddenly attacked the officer in charge.*"

"*Wow, that's crazy! Is the officer alright?*"

"*I'm guessing so. He was treated at the scene.*"

"*So what did they do with the body? Is it the same guy they were talking about on the news?*"

"*As far as I know, yes, and it's waiting assessment in the morgue. David's been busy trying to process the ones from before…*"

She could still hear the sound of their voices, but beyond that, wasn't able to make out anything else they said. They had either moved further away or had considerably lowered the volume of their voices.

As she is trying to hear the rest of the nurse's conversation, she suddenly yawns, and while stretching she feels a dull pain in her chest and right leg. As she runs her hands down to inspect them at the source, she finds that she is heavily bandaged around her chest, while the wound from her right leg is currently uncovered. The fingers of her right hand slowly follow the path of stitches across her leg, easily more than a hundred, and she marvels at how she is even alive.

Her last image had been of John's face leaning down over hers. She had placed her hand over his cheek, trying to comfort him in what she had believed to be her last moments. There was no reason for her to think otherwise. Her life blood poured from what should have been mortal wounds. She had felt herself growing distant and cold with each beat of the very heart that had been pierced by the instrument in her chest.

"Oh hun, I'm so sorry," she whispered to the memory of John's face. "I never meant to hurt you."

Her eyes filled with tears of her own as she recalled the last moments of the battle at The Clothing Store.

Draegan, the vampire they had come searching for, had emerged from the heart of the store, and even though she was in the midst of her own battle, she had looked over to lay her eyes upon the creature for the second time in her life.

The first time they had fought the creature, she had been in her mid-twenties. She was at the top of her game and ready for anything. This time, however, she'd had to fight with every ounce of strength and energy she could muster. She was still in excellent shape, and one would be hard pressed to place her out of her thirties, but the truth was she was nowhere near as fast as she used to be.

In the two seconds that she had spent looking upon the face of the beast, she had also seen two of the goons in overalls sneaking up behind Quinn. He'd

146

*continued reading the verses John had written for him
and if she hadn't been in such an urgent battle, she
might have beamed from ear to ear in pride. For the
first time since she had met him, he spoke with
confidence and without faltering. His voice was strong
and pure, and he channeled every bit of goodness in him
through those words and at the creature now sailing
through the air at J.R.*

*She watched as he finished reading from his notebook
and placed it into his breast pocket. Two sets of arms
suddenly grabbed him from behind, and if she hadn't felt
the icy heat of the weapon piercing her chest, she might
have been able to call out a warning. All she managed
was a cry of pain, which had then been abruptly cut
short by her sudden loss for breath. She turned her
attention back to her attackers and fired several shots
in rapid succession, taking them down with her.*

The memories tore at her already weakened heart,
breaking it even further at the thought of her friend's
suffering. It had been hard enough when they had lost
Brody, but here she awakens, alone, with the memory of
Quinn being taken by the monster's jobbers. Here she
awakens with the last image of her beloved John looking
upon her, tears rolling down his ageless features, and
with his soul breaking behind those magnificent grey-
gold orbs.

The pain is too much for her to bear, and for the
first time in her life, she has an emotional breakdown.
She is overcome with a feeling of hopelessness so strong
that her small frame shakes with each sob, and it is a
long time before the grief passes.

Sometime later, she awakens to the sound of rushing
footsteps outside her door. She comes to with a start,
surprised that she wasn't aware of having fallen asleep,
and from the outside of her room she can hear voices
speaking with an extreme sense of urgency.

"Sir? Sir, can you tell me your name?"
"There's no response. Nurse, is there a pulse?"
"Yes doctor, but it's faint."

147

"Quickly, get him prepped for surgery. There might still be enough time to save this arm..."

They must have stopped at the nurse's station outside of her room to check in the patient and this was why she had been able to hear them. The further down the hall they traveled, the harder it was for her to hear what they were saying. Soon, it was calm once more and she pulled herself up and into a sitting position. It was painful to move, but she found that if she was careful enough, she could do it.

Reaching off to the side, she searched until she found what she was looking for; the button to call a nurse. Taking it into her left hand, she pressed it and waited.

It was several minutes before the door opened, but it wasn't a nurse who stepped inside. She was surprised at first, but when her eyes adjusted to the light, she calmed as she realized that the person was wearing a blue uniform.

"I hope you don't mind my intrusion. Your nurse left her station to help with another patient."

His voice was deep, soothing, and it immediately put at her at ease.

"Do you mind," he asked as he reached for the light dimmer.

"No, please," she answered.

He turned the dial slightly and the lights brightened from within several recessed cups in the ceiling. They were dim, they did very little to chase away the shadows, but it did give her a chance to finally see the man speaking to her without any trouble.

He was easily taller than her John, who was just over six feet tall. He was also very muscular, and she was reminded instantly of a former Californian Governor when he had once appeared as Conan the Barbarian on the big screen. As big as he was, he still moved with the grace of someone half his size.

His uniform was form fitting and she blushed when she realized that she had been undressing him with her eyes. He had a policeman's cap tucked under one arm, suggesting that he had only just arrived, but something

148

about the way he looked at her suggested that he had already been in to see her. He looked only at her, rather than around the room as would have been her first instinct.

He had the chiseled features of an eighties action hero, but not in the kind of way which seemed wooden. When he smiled, she found herself feeling both protected and loved at the same time, and she felt as if she could easily get lost in the sea of his dark blue eyes.

There was something else about him as well, something that she hadn't thought of since the last time she had been to the hotel. The same thing she had felt about her John, she could sense surrounding this man as well. Only, with this ebony haired stranger, the aura of power surrounding him spoke of more things than just the holy promise of J.R.'s. With this stranger's, she could sense all of eternity surrounding him.

"How are you feeling," he asked as he stepped fully into the room.

"I, uh… Surprisingly good?"

"I'm sorry, I should have introduced myself. My name is Michael."

He extended his left hand, and she was shocked to realize that it was so much larger that hers seemed like a child's inside of it. He didn't shake her hand, but rather, held onto it for a moment before releasing it.

"I'm…"

"Chloe Grace Hudson, oldest daughter of Phillip and Linnie Hudson, both of whom were mysteriously killed when you were eight. You bounced from home to home before finally running away at the age of twelve. While riding in the boxcar of a southbound train, you met a stranger who would change the course of your life forever. He took you under his wing, so to speak, teaching you how to protect yourself against the evils of humanity, as well as against thing far less human."

"That's right, but how-"

"You traveled with this stranger of the night, learning his secrets and fighting at his side for the next ten years, until the night that you gave yourself to him fully. The next morning he was gone, and you

149

wouldn't see him again until five years later, when you would arrive at a certain diner-"

"That's enough, damn it! How could you possibly know all of this? There is only one other person whom I have shared every detail with, and he's-"

"He's not that far away and he's fighting for his life even as we speak."

"I, I don't understand. Just who in the hell are you?"

"Not hell, Chloe, but I'm surprised that you have to ask."

When she only offered a confused expression, he just smiled warmly in return. His was a look of such warmth and compassion that her worries instantly melted. It no longer mattered how he knew her most intimate secrets, nor did she have any fears as to how they would be used.

"I'm sorry, Officer."

"Just Michael, is fine," he gently corrected her.

"Alright then, Michael," she offered, testing it out. Only when his smile reassured her that this was okay did she continue.

"Quinn? He's here?"

Before he could answer, there was another commotion outside. Several feet pounded past the room in the same direction that the gurney had traveled earlier.

"I'm afraid I can't say anything more. I must be going."

He turned to leave and had gotten several steps closer to the door before she stopped him.

"Wait! Do you know anything about my stranger of the night?"

Without turning around, he placed his cap on his head and used both hands to level it before answering.

"I'm afraid he's gone."

The words sent a cold chill through her very core.

"What!? You mean he's-?"

"Yes, but it's not too late."

"Wait," she called out as he placed his hand on the door to push it open. "What does that mean?"

"Have faith, Chloe Hudson, and the rest will take care of itself."

With that, he pushed the door open and stepped outside. The door slowly closed behind him, leaving her with more questions than she had answers. Just who was this stranger, and how is it that he seemed to know so much? Once he was gone, her worries and fears crept back into the room, surrounding her as she questioned the reality of her strange visit.

"Did that just happen?"

Just then the door opened and a nurse entered the room. She was older than Chloe and had a very matronly look about her. Her silvery hair was coiled up in a bun on top of her head, but wisps of hair had recently escaped and hung down around the aged features of her face.

Though she was out of breath, she smiled as she entered the room and turned the dimmer back to where it had been before.

"There we go now dear, did you call for me?"

"Y-yes, I suppose I did," she stammered. She had forgotten about pressing the call button just moments before her visit with Michael. "You didn't, um- You didn't just see a police officer leave my room did you?"

"No? I'm just returning from the E.R. I think I would have noticed someone leaving your room. Why do you ask?"

"Oh, it's nothing," she said quietly. "Is there any way I could get something to eat? I'm starving!"

The nurse smiled at her as she finished approaching her bedside. She stood just off to her right, where there were machines monitoring her progress, and for perhaps the first time since waking she realized that there were wires attached to her via IV, as well as several others for monitoring her heart.

"Everything seems to be fine here," the nurse murmured. "We were really surprised when the ambulance arrived, you know. David had pronounced you dead at the scene, but when you got to us, your wounds were closed and you had a faint heartbeat."

She spoke more to herself than directly to Chloe, and when she was finished, her eyes wandered up to a simple cross which hung on the wall.

"It really is a miracle, you know?"

151

Chloe didn't know how to respond. She was tired, weary from the inside-out, and didn't have the energy to think about the implications behind her being here.

"But listen to me, babbling on about miracles and such. You're starving, you poor thing!"
The nurse, whose name-tag identified her as Marissa, slipped her left hand under Chloe's right, and placed her right over the top.

"What can I get for you dear? The kitchen is closed, but I'd be happy to call something in for you?"

Chloe smiled, relieved that she would be able to get something tonight.

"I'd be grateful for a sandwich and a salad, if that's possible?"

"It certainly is," she answered with a smile. "How are you feeling," she asked as she checked the bandages.

"There's a dull ache where my injuries are, but-"

The nurse gasped when she looked beneath the bandages around her chest.

"What? What is it," she asked fearfully.

"I've never seen anything like this," was the only explanation she got.

"You just rest dear. I'm going to call the doctor to come and look at you while I see to it that you get something in your tummy tonight."

She patted the top of Chloe's right hand before she left, but it did nothing to ease the discomfort her reaction had caused. What had she seen to give her the sudden need to leave the room? She pulled her gown open and looked down at the bandages, but there weren't any answers on the outside. Except, that wasn't true was it? When was the last time her bandages had been changed? There should be blood soaking into them, even *if* the wound were mostly closed.

Her thoughts were distracted by a tickling in her right leg, one which reminded her of the feeling one gets before looking down to see a bug crawling on them. Because she was partially sitting, inspecting the source of this curious feeling was as simple as turning her attention downward. What she saw was nothing short of a miracle. The stitches were falling out of the wound on her leg, which had miraculously healed into an angry pink scar!

"What is going on here," she murmured.

She quickly looked around the room, suddenly interested in where her personal belongings might be. To her left was a small couch, just big enough for two people to sit on, a plush chair, and an end table centered between the two. Past the foot of her bed, and on the wall to the left of the door, was a small dresser. The wall to the right of the door was connected with the wall to the right of her bed by simple shelving, upon which are instruments used by the nurses and doctors while attending to their patients. The corner, from the floor to about four feet up, is built into a cabinet, out of which she can see a faucet, hand sanitizing wash, and other hygienic products.

The wall on the right is occupied only by a small table, upon which is a vase of roses much like the ones in the bouquet next to her bed. There is a door to the right of her head and she can just see the edge of a bath on the end of it.

"Miracle or not, I've got to see if Quinn is alright," she growled defiantly.

With one last look at the door, she begins plucking the monitoring devices from her chest and sides, then, taking a deep breath, she removes the IV and swings her legs over the side of the bed. The alarms on the equipment immediately begin going off and she quickly finds the power switch to monitor and flicks it off.

Nurse Marissa might not be far away, and she didn't particularly want to be here when she returned. While there might not be anything but good intentions, there was too much at stake for her to just lie around while they fuss over her recovery.

She eased herself to the floor and found that her leg, while suffering the tingles from having been in one position for too long, supported her without any problem. She quickly crossed the room to the dresser and looked inside, but it was empty.

"Damn! I guess I'm going to have to do this the hard way."

She pulled her robe closed and secured it as best as she could, which wasn't saying much, before stepping to the side of the door. When she was satisfied that there was nobody on the other side, she opened it a crack and peeked through.

From her angle, she could see the edge of the nurse's station fifteen feet away but there was nobody there. She could hear a faint beeping, likely their end of the monitoring equipment, coming from there, and knew that it wouldn't be long before she was discovered. Opening the door a little further, she stuck her head out and looked in both directions.

To the left, the hall continued for another thirty feet. There were doors on either side of the hall, presumably leading into rooms similar to hers, before it turned abruptly to the right. To the right of her room, and past the nurse's station, there was a set of double doors leading into another section of the hospital.

Taking a deep breath, she opened the door and stepped out into the hall. She would have to find a way out of here and the only way she knew how would be to first go into the heart of danger itself.

Keeping her back against the wall, she began to close the distance between her and the nurse's station. She stopped to check the doors as she passed them. In the event that someone returned while she wandered down the hall, she wanted to have a temporary backup plan in place. This proved to be unnecessary, however, when she reached the small desk with no encounters.

Just as she had hoped for, nobody was there. The computer screen beeped regularly as it relayed the same alarm she had silenced from her room. A quick glance at the monitor showed a flatline on Jane Doe, room 103. She could hear the sound of voices approaching and it wouldn't be long before one, or both nurses stationed here, returned.

"Damn," she muttered. "There's got to be some way I can buy myself some time."

She could see that the double doors were just a few feet away, but there wasn't any way to block them off.

"That's no good anyway," she muttered. "That'd raise the alarms faster than anything else."

She noticed there was a volume button on the side of the monitor. Placing her finger over the minus symbol, she pressed down until there was no longer any sound, and she prayed that nothing befell the fates of the other patients this system was monitoring.

"This will have to do."

From the other side of the doors, she could just hear the conversation of the nurses as they returned. They were talking about how their newest patient was lucky to be alive. If she could hear them, it wouldn't be long before they walked through those doors and saw her leaning over the desk.

"Damn! Not enough time," she cursed.

She was going to have to take her chances down the other direction. With one last look around, and not before taking a framed printout showing her location, she ran past her room and to the ninety-degree turn at the end of the hall. Her flight was frantic, and the carpet concealed most of the sound from her passage, but it still wasn't going to be enough.

Behind her, where she had only moments ago had been looking through the nurse's station, she heard a high pitched buzz indicating that the double doors were being opened. If they were looking ahead while they walked, there would be no mistaking what was happening. They would see the exposed backside of their nameless patient, fleeing as though the very hounds of hell were chasing her.

XIII

NOWHERE TO HIDE

114, 116, 118… The doors rushed past as she continued to sprint down the hall. They had seen her, and while they might not be chasing her, her chances of getting out of here without incident were gone. She paused against the door to room 124 to look at the floor design. According to the layout, there should be a pair of elevators to the left at an upcoming 'T' intersection.

"She went that way," called the voice of the nurse Marissa, who had just been in her room.

"Shit," she cursed in frustration.

It hadn't taken long for security to get here, which meant that she had even less time to find a way out of this situation.

"What would John do," she asked desperately.

She could hear the guards rapidly closing the distance to her, and groaned. Though her wounds had mysteriously healed after the Sergeant had visited her, her body was still weak from exertion. Each breath she took burned and her leg shook weakly beneath under her weight.

"…not gonna make it," she muttered.

She reached behind her with her left hand, feeling for the handle to the door.

"Please be unlocked," she prayed hopefully.

The handle went down and the door cracked open behind her.

"Thank God," she said as she slipped into the room. Not a moment too soon, for as she closed the door behind her, the guards thundered past. She watched from the darkness of the room, peering through the small peephole as two heavy set rent-a-cops lumbered past.

"Hello?" called a voice from behind her. "Is somebody there?"

She turned around, quickly placing her back to the door, but she couldn't see anything. The voice had only been that of a little girl, however, and she sounded scared.

"I'm sorry hun; I must have the wrong room."

"Please don't go. Mommy went home to sleep tonight and I'm all alone."

"Well," She stretched the word out, the universal way of implying that one had something else one would rather be doing.

"Pretty please? Just until I go to sleep?"

Chloe sighed and turned the dimmer switch on just that she could see. The room was set up much like her own, except there were two chairs near the end of the bed, the latter which was also considerably smaller than hers had been. Lying in the center of the bed was a small child about the size of an eight year old. She couldn't be sure of her age, however, because the child was completely wrapped in bandages.

"You don't have to stay if you don't want to," she said dejectedly. "I heard you sigh."

"Oh no, it's not that at all," she said while crossing the room. As she walked, she tied the gown closed behind her. "It's just that I'm in a bit of trouble and if I stay in one place for too long it could get a whole lot worse."

"A-are you a bad person?"

"No, or, at least I don't think I am. But there are some people who might think otherwise."

She sat down in a plush chair by the headboard and folded her hands in her lap.

"Why?"

"Well, it's complicated."

This time it was the girl who sighed.

"I'm not stupid you know. Just because I'm a kid, doesn't mean that I can't handle the truth."

Chloe was taken aback and didn't know exactly how to respond.

"My name's Dana, what's yours?"

"Chloe. It's a pleasure to meet you Dana."

"Same. Now Chloe, are you going to tell me why someone would think you're a bad person?"

"Well, like I said, it's complicated. Do you know anything about what's been going on in the news?"

"Yes?" She answered slowly, drawing at the word in an unsure tone.

"Then you have probably heard about what happened at *The Clothing Store* on the edge of town then, right?"

The girl was silent for several moments before answering and Chloe became fearful that she might be deciding as to whether or not to call for help.

"Are you the girl they say was helping 'Him'?"

"Maybe…" It was her turn to answer with an unsure tone. "That depends on the 'Him' you are talking about."

"You know, the guy who they're saying killed a lot of people?"

"Yeah," she answered with a sigh. "I guess I'm her."

"But, they said you died."

"I think I kinda did, hun," she replied.

There was another long pause as Dana seemed to chew this over. This time it was Chloe who broke the silence.

"How did this happen to you?"

"We had an accident in our car and I was thrown out the window. The doctors said that it's a miracle I survived, but-"

"But?"

"Well, I don't know if I should tell you. Mommy got mad when I told her, and she said that I shouldn't talk about it anymore."

"Dana, can I ask something?"

"Yeah."

"Why haven't you called the nurse yet, or called for help?"

"It's complicated," she answered playfully. Her lips, the only part of her face that was visible, moved upward into an ornery smile.

"You don't have to worry about me getting mad, hun. I seriously doubt that anything you tell me will shock or surprise me."

The girl seemed to mull it over, and once again the room was filled with silence. Beyond the soft beeping of her monitoring equipment, nothing more was said between the two for several minutes. During that time, there was more plenty more activity outside of the room. A small group of personnel passed down the halls,

158

discussing the possibility that she might have ducked into one of the rooms.

Chloe watched the door with concern, hoping that, if they started going from room to room, that they wouldn't start here. If they did, she didn't see how she was going to get away.

"The last thing I remember was getting out of my seat to pick up my MP3 player. Then, there was darkness. It was so cold and I kept calling for Mommy, but she wasn't answering. Then, there was this light. It was so bright, and when I tried to close my eyes, I couldn't. The light was everywhere. It kept getting brighter and brighter. I was so scared. Then the light wasn't so bright, and there 'he' was."

"He?"

"An angel," she answered reverently. "He was SOOO big! Bigger than those wrestlers you see on TV!"

"What did he look like," Chloe asked thoughtfully. An idea was beginning to form in her head, but she wanted to hear it from her, first.

"He looked like King Arthur! He wore shiny armor, and on top of it was this thing that kinda looked like a shirt, but it didn't have sides. And on the front was the picture of a cross with two swords behind it like the letter 'X'. And he had the bluest eyes I had ever seen!"

Chloe only partially listened as the girl excitedly prattled on. She was beginning to see the picture more and more clearly, and the revelation was startling.

"He also had the longest and blackest hair I had ever seen for a boy! And, he had this huge sword on his back. I know it was huge because the part that you hold onto was above his head, but the point was behind his knees. Also, he had the most beautiful wings! They were so white and so big!"

Chloe could picture every detail Dana recounted. It was easy because she had seen him not too long ago in her own room. Only, he had been wearing a police uniform, and he hadn't had wings.

"He told me that he needed me to do something for him."

"Do you remember what he said?"

"Uh-huh. He asked me to be strong. He told me it was going to hurt for a while, but there was going to be someone who would need my help. He said that if I helped that person, she would go on to save a lot of people. He also said that if I wasn't there, she would die and so would everyone else."

She sat in stunned silence while Dana spoke. By all accounts, Dana had been given the opportunity to be here so that she would be safe!

"Did the angel tell you his name," she asked.

"He didn't have to. I know him from the windows at church. His name is Michael."

Chloe's mind reeled from the answer. Her thoughts flashed back to the last time she had been in the motel.

After she hands him the Glock .22s, John removes a small diamond tipped tool from his satchel and begins etching the symbol of St. Michael into the butt of each pistol. He works expertly, is done within minutes of starting, and he smiles as he returns her newly blessed tools.

"John," she gasps, "they're beautiful! Who is he?"

On each pistol he had drawn two different versions of the saint.

"He is known as St. Michael, the archangel and patron of battles and war. His is the hand of God and he who deals divine justice upon the enemy. Allow him into your heart, that he may protect you in the battle to come."

"Hello? Are you still here?"

"Y-yeah. Sorry hun, I was thinking."

"About what?"

"About your angel. Michael? I think he visited me today."

"He's nice, isn't he?"

"Yeah, he sure is."

Nothing more was said between the two and after several minutes Chloe stood up to leave.

"Chloe?"

"Yeah?"

"Thank you."

"For what?"

"For being kind. I'm sorry that I can't see you, but
I don't think I shall ever forget what you sound like."

"I won't forget you either, Dana. I hope that
someday we can meet under better circumstances."

She leaned forward and placed a gentle kiss at the
corner of the girl's mouth, then reclined in the chair
until she was sure that Dana had fallen asleep.

Moving quietly, so as to not disturb her, she crossed
the room and put her eye up to the peephole. The first
thing she noticed was the two guards standing at each
end of the hall. The second was her nurse, entering the
room across from her with a third security guard, this
one armed.

What am I going to do," she thought. *"There's
nowhere to hide!"*

She turned around and put her back to the door, a
scene not unlike the one before she found her way in
here, and look around the room. The lights were dim,
but they were just enough for her to see the one
difference this room had from hers. On the wall
opposite of where she stood was a window that looked
like it was just big enough for her to slip through.

"Just great," she grumbled.

Pushing off of the door, she sprinted across the room
in six strides. The window was the kind that opened
much like a laundry chute, and she would have to climb
up and step down through it in order to get out. She
was in the process of doing this when the door began to
open behind her.

Very much like the proverbial deer caught in the
headlights, she froze with half of her body out the
window. All she had to do was duck her head down and
pull her other leg through, but she just couldn't make
herself do it. It was as if time, at least for her, was
standing still. A light breeze blew in from the
outside, gently lifting her hair up and around the sides
of her head. It also rippled through her gown and sent
a chill down her spine.

As the security guard stepped into the room, she saw
that she had one saving grace for freedom and it spurred
her into motion. He was carrying a flashlight over

161

handed, with the beam pointed at the floor and just a few feet in front of him. There were only a couple seconds to react before he looked up and saw her straddling the open window, and without further thought, she used one of them to escape.

She was one story above the ground with only six inches of concrete ledge to stand on. It was still dark outside, and as if that wasn't enough, a light rain made her situation even more precarious. Without wasting any more time, she began sliding herself in the direction of a window, to a room they had already searched, and with any luck she would find it open.

The time it was taking to increase the distance between herself and Dana's room was agonizingly slow, and each time she slid her foot just a little closer to the next window, she expected it to slip out from under her. Though she was only a story above the ground, the beckoning sea of asphalt promised her a more permanent stay if she were to fall.

Now soaked from the rain, her gown offered her little protection from the cool night air. The combination only intensified her discomfort, reminding her that she had to find a way off of this ledge, and quickly! As if this wasn't incentive enough, the window she had just come through closed and she heard the click of a lock being bolted from the inside.

"At least no one thought to look out here," she murmured. Her words were snatched away by the wind, greedily sucked into the air and silenced before even she had a chance to hear them.

The window to the next room was only a couple feet from where she stood. She could almost reach it if she stretched! She turned herself slightly to the side, slowly easing herself down as she reached forward to check if the window were open. At that moment, however, a pair of headlights turned toward the building from the other side of the parking lot below.

If whoever was driving had been looking up, she knew that she had to have been spotted, and what a sight she would be! Crouched on a ledge, one story above the ground, a seemingly naked woman reaching toward a window!

Closer inspection showed that she didn't have anything to worry about. The car swerved erratically back and forth as the driver tried to shake a ghostly passenger clinging to the hood. There were no other lights in the parking lot, and it was difficult for her to make out any details, but it seemed there was someone or something trying to fight its way in. The car pitched to the right, and just as quickly, the hitchhiker scurried in the opposite direction across the hood.

There were suddenly two small explosions from the cab of the vehicle as a large gun discharged and her heart skipped a beat when she recognized the sound.

"John," she breathed.

The revelation came with little joy. The flash from the gun had shown the true nature of the hitchhiker.

Clawing frantically at the hood was something that looked like a werewolf. Instead of being large and muscular, however, this creature was slender and had long one long pointed ear atop its head. Its fur was the color of snow, which explained why it had looked so ghostly from afar, and there seemed to be big patches missing from one side. John must have really worked him over!

There was another small explosion, from the car's interior, as the passenger fired again. The creature yelped in pain and when the car next swerved, it tumbled from the hood and rolled several times across the ground before coming to a stop. The car also skidded to a stop, sliding sideways so that the creature was in the beams.

From her vantage, she could just make out the form of a small man sitting behind the wheel.

"Quinn," she mouthed with a puzzled expression on her face.

It didn't feel right. Michael had said that he was fighting for his life, but he had also implied that her friend was already here as well. So how was it that he was behind the wheel of the car below and here at the same time?

Try as she might, she couldn't see any other details other than the shape of his face. The rain was falling heavier now, and it was with great difficulty that was able to even see the creature. Wisps of fog rose from the ground, giving the illusion that the ground had suddenly become warmer than it really was.

She watched as the passenger in the cab opened the door and stood next to the car. Just beneath the sound of the rain, she heard the driver as he called out to his friend.

"You must wear this as well. It will do no good unless we complete the illusion!"

The figure standing next to the car leaned over as he took something from the interior. When he next stood, he was wearing a hat that she knew all too well.

"Complete the illusion," she asked. "Did I hear that correctly?"

She watched as J.R. walked to the front of the car. His duster billowed around him, and there was no reason for her to believe otherwise, but her instincts told her that something was not right.

John lifted his left hand, palm facing outward toward the creature, as he continued his approach. The wind screeched in her ears, as it ran off the sides of the building, but it didn't completely drown out the words of a prayer she had come to know so well over the years.

Her legs began to tremble beneath her as they weakened from the continuous effort. She had been on the ledge for several minutes now, crouching from her attempt to examine a window she had long forgotten. Though she had only been awake for a short time, her body threatened to betray her.

So many questions ran through her mind, and there would be many more before she found her way back inside, but for now she had to face her own perils. She pressed in on the window, sighing with relief when it lowered enough for her to enter, and with one last look over her shoulder she climbed back into the building.

As the speaker's voice rose in volume, she saw a familiar golden glow beginning to form, around John's hand? For that matter, why was Quinn reciting the litany? It didn't make sense, but she didn't have time to watch the outcome. She needed to get off this ledge.

Even as the confrontation outside continued to build to a head, she stepped fully through the window and fell ungracefully to the floor inside. The room was dark, but enough light trickled in beneath the door that she was able to see the shape of a bed next to her. It appeared to have been recently vacated, as the sheets were pulled away and piled to one side, but a quick survey of the room revealed that for the moment she was alone.

A monstrous roar echoed up from the parking lot outside and she cringed involuntarily. It was a powerful sound, evil, and it spoke of dark promises better left unimagined. She shivered partially from the cold, and partially from the fear of what those promises spoke of, and she could only think of getting as far away from the sound as possible.

Her mind was gripped in terror during the few seconds that the beast howled, forcing her into retreat. She turned around, all thoughts of her pursuers forgotten, and bolted for the door. The beast roared again, this time from farther away, but her will wasn't yet strong enough to register the difference. She had never faced anything like this before, even when at her John's side, and her mind simply wasn't ready to come to terms with it on any level.

She looked over her shoulder, her terrified eyes bulging from their sockets, and promptly lost her balance. She had forgotten about the water dripping from her gown, and hadn't noticed as it collected at her feet. She stumbled forward a few steps, partially running, partially falling, before the inevitable caught up with her. She hit the floor with a resounding *splat!*

The anguished cries of the beast had ceased, but only outside of her head. Its effects, on the other hand, continued to serve its age old purpose; to instill unholy terror unto those who heard it.

XIV

A PRIEST, AN EX-COP AND THE BLONDE

Jonesy stood next to the car, shaking from the aftermath of the battle. All at once, he was a rookie all over again, except this time he had no training with which to fall upon. This was something beyond his realm of understanding. He had never in his wildest dreams thought that he would be battling vampires, let alone werewolves, and yet here he was; filling the shoes of a man built for this very destiny.

"I believe it is gone, my young friend. We must hurry! If what he said to you was true, we don't have much time."

The old priest clambered weakly out of the car. His skin was pale and he shook as much from exhaustion as he did the exertion of the night's battles. Jonesy watched him with great concern. He knew that he shouldn't have brought him; his every instinct screamed that the danger was too great, but he couldn't deny that the man had been more than helpful tonight. If it wasn't for his spiritual strength, he knew he would have fallen long before reaching this point.

Ezra reached into the car and removed the final item from the bottom of the backpack.

"Take this. Something tells me that he'll want all of his things once he returns."

"I still don't know about all this," Jonesy said doubtfully. "I… I think I can get used to the idea of there being a Dracula. I'm also sure that I can handle the fact that I've fought off some of his uglier spawn. I think I can even accept that that creature was a werewolf. But-"

"But what?"

"I don't know. When John touched my arm, he somehow touched my mind as well. I can't explain it exactly, but for a moment I suddenly knew everything he knew."

"Really now? Everything?"

"Well, no. He showed me memories of his childhood. I learned about how to be a hunter just as sure as if I was there with him. He also showed me the faces of those closest to him-"

When Jonesy trailed off in thought, Ezra prompted him to continue.

"Go on."

As they were talking, they had begun walking toward the hospital.

"I was just thinking. The faces he showed me were of his closest and dearest friends. Two of those he showed me were associated with grisly scenes in which one was decapitated and dismembered, while the other bled out in his arms from a mortal wound to her chest."

"Yes? Why do you think this was important?"

"I'm not sure. I don't even think he meant to show me. He was full of so much grief…" he involuntarily sucked in his breath as an empathetic wave of emotion nearly overcame him.

"It's okay Lachlan. I don't think I ever got used to it either."

"You mean… He's shown you as well?"

"Not exactly, it was more of a feeling than the images you describe. Each time I felt them, it was as if the weight of a million souls had fallen onto my shoulders."

Jonesy paused at the entrance to the hospital. They had been so engrossed in their conversation that neither had noticed the lights go out on the first level. They were only out for a second, and by the time that they had made it to the entrance, the emergency lights had flickered to life.

"Before we go in, I think there's something else we have to do while we're here."

Ezra raised an eyebrow.

"As we were walking up to the hospital, I saw a woman looking down at us from the second story."

"I don't understand, what does this have to do with our current task?"

"It was the woman who died in his arms, or rather; John seems to think she died. I want to find her before we do whatever it is we're supposed to do at the Morgue."

Jonesy looked down at his shorter friend, his eyes hidden under the shadow of J.R.'s hat, and placed a hand onto the man's shoulder.

167

"Are you sure you're up for this?"

"There is no choice my friend. Dracula has come, lycanthropes attack in the open, and the dead have risen. With all that you have told me, and all that we have seen, there has to be something we can do for John. You wouldn't have been sent a messenger if there wasn't."

Jonesy squeezed his friend's shoulder comfortingly. He was right of course. The Asian man HAD been some sort of messenger, and he was beyond arguing or trying to explain otherwise.

"I'm frightened," he whispered in a childlike voice. "Father, will you pray for me?"

"Certainly, my son."

And so they prayed as they stood outside of the hospital entrance. It was a prayer that J.R. would have recognized and approved of, as it was the very one he used before every coming battle. When his spiritual strength had finally failed him, he had passed the words on to Quinn, who in turn had used them in the battle against Draegan, and Ezra had just moments before used them against the Jackal. Once they were finished, they turned and entered the hospital doors.

Jonesy's instincts told him immediately that something was wrong. The interior was bathed in the red glow of emergency lights and the air reeked of something he did not at first recognize. They stood in the reception hall of the hospital, a large rectangular room with a 'C' shaped desk large enough, and fitted for, three secretaries. There were two hallways splitting off the desk and leading deeper into the hospital, but nowhere in front of them did they see anything to suggest that anyone was around.

"I don't like the looks of this," Jonesy said with trepidation as they looked around the room.

He reached down and pulled the duster open to reveal Jessie, which was now holstered at his right hip. Just as they did in the movies, he pulled the material of the duster back behind the weapon in case he needed to quickly draw it. Mentally, he was the man with no name, about to do battle with a few dozen banditos. He felt powerful enough to take on the worst 'they' had to throw at him.

"Look!"

The old man had interrupted his thoughts just in time. A nurse stumbled around the corner at the end of the left hallway. Her head was down, seemingly studying the floor, as she continued her slow approach. She was dressed in what appeared to be dark blue scrubs, but beneath the red glow of the lights it was difficult to tell. What he did notice was the darker stain around her midsection, a stain which had spread down her left leg.

Her steps were slow and deliberate, and even after he called out to her, she continued to watch the floor rather than acknowledge their presence. When there was only ten feet between them, she fell forward, first onto her knees, and then onto her face.

They looked at one another, both silently agreeing on what they had to do next. A quick sprint closed the distance to the nurse, whom now lay in a pool of growing blood. Jonesy knew before checking for her pulse that she was gone, the large hole in the middle of her back showed him all that he had needed to see. It was a miracle that she had even gotten this far! Ezra turned her head to the side and drew a cross on her cheek with holy water as he issued her forth to the next world.

"We're not going to have time to do that for everyone we come across," Jonesy said as his friend finished.

"Perhaps, but if I hadn't done that for this one she would have continued running long after her death."

Jonesy nodded, but didn't say anything further on the subject. He watched the corner at the end of the hall, from which this poor woman had stumbled, and wondered what had done this to her.

"Quickly," Ezra urged. "Let us find this woman you spoke of."

Around the corner was a sight more grisly than what either of the men was prepared to witness. It was another long hallway, at the end of which were two double doors. Littered on the floor were the remains of several other victims, most of whom were less fortunate than the nurse they left behind them. They began

169

picking their way through the bodies, careful not to slip in the blood beneath their feet.

They first passed what might have been a security guard. He was seated against the wall with his legs splayed out in front of him. His right hand still held onto a flashlight which had been broken during his final struggle. The left hung broken at his side, while his face was unrecognizable as ever being human.

Beyond the guard they passed the first pair of rooms, one directly across from the other. Whatever had done this hadn't neglected to stop in each one during its murderous rampage. In the room to their right they could only see the victim's feet sticking past the foot of the bed on the floor. Blood covered the wall opposite the door where the body had fallen.

The room to the left was even worse. It only took a second to determine what had happened to the poor person in there. The victim had been torn to shreds. Pieces of flesh were thrown against the walls, where they either slid down or stuck where they landed, while larger chunks littered the floor all across the room.

Moving on, they passed the body of another security guard. This one lay on the ground with the back of his head touching his ankles, a look of surprise forever frozen on his face. He had gotten so far as to remove his gun from its holster, but whatever had done this to him had been much faster.

"Oh dear God," Ezra choked.

"Maybe we shouldn't check every room," Jonesy answered weakly. He was looking into the next room on the right, inside of which had been a small family. He was fortunate to not see the faces of the bodies, but what he did see in the carnage would haunt him for the rest of his life. Just to the left and inside the room, a door was cracked open. On the floor inside was the small hand of a child reaching for a doll just inches away. Three of the child's fingers had been bitten clean off, leaving behind only the thumb and forefinger.

He quickly shut the door, before Ezra could see what was on the other side of it, and turned his attention to the double doors at the end of the hall. They picked their way through the debris of human flesh for what seemed like hours, carefully placing their footing where they could.

When it felt as if their sanity could take no more, they had reached the end of the death tunnel. The last two rooms were ten feet behind them, with only blank wall between there and where they now stood. A small floor plan, taped on the right-hand door, suggested they would enter an intersection where two halls met. From there and to their right would be a pair of elevators.

"There," Jonesy said, tapping the location of the elevators. "It shouldn't be far."

Ezra only nodded. The smaller man was staring back into the hall they had just traversed. His eyes had a glazed look in them, a look that Jonesy now recognized all too well. Taking him by the elbow, he turned and opened the left of the two doors, pulling him into what lay beyond.

"Come on, not now," he pled to the despondent priest. "Not you!"

This side of the hallway was thankfully clear of bodies, and the only blood that he could see was from the tracks that their feet were now leaving. He moved in front of his companion and searched his eyes for several seconds before speaking.

"Come on, old friend. This isn't the best time for this," he said nervously. There was no response, however. Only the same glassy stare.

"Damn it!"

He continued forward, leading the old man by the elbow as quickly as he could, but the going was slow and the intersection didn't seem to be getting any closer. There were some doors to their right and left, none exactly opposite of one another, and each one was locked. It wasn't until they reached the intersection that he saw what he needed.

To the right were the elevators, but to the left were a pair of doors that were standing wide open. They were offices, most likely for doctors on call, but they had both been abandoned in the wake of the attack. He led Ezra into the closest one and shut the door behind them. It was small, accommodating only a desk and a couple of chairs, but it was what he needed for now. Sweeping

171

everything off of the desk, he led Ezra over and guided him on top of it, laying him flat on his back. Using a couple of books, he propped the older man's feet up before taking a quick look back into the hall.

His heart was conflicted. How could he leave behind a man whom he had known most of his life, a man who wore the cloth and spoke for the Lord, for a man he had only known for less than twenty-four hours? Especially after the carnal destruction they had just left behind? But the thought was there. He knew that he would have to make a decision very soon if things didn't change.

He didn't see anything in the hallway, but then again, peeking through the crack offered a very limited view in either direction. As quietly as he could, he shut the door and threw the lock. While he knew that he was very pressed for time, he also couldn't proceed unless he was sure of his decision. Twice tonight, Ezra had nearly succumbed to a medical condition that had been brought on by the events around them. What if the next time it happens, he's not there to help him? What if whatever is out there gets ahold of him and he CAN'T help him?

As if to answer his last question, an inhuman growl echoed from deep in the bowels of the hospital. It was shortly followed by the scream of the creature's next victim.

Could it be that the werewolf had found a way into the hospital before they had? If that was the case, then he was responsible for all of this. The blood of these victims would forever be on his hands unless he was able to put it down.

A part of him tried to put blame of the lycanthrope's appearance upon J.R.'s shoulders. When the beast had first attacked, it had mistaken him for the man whose clothes he now wore. Twice before reaching the hospital, however, it had snarled the name of another. While the beast had known of J.R., he didn't think that it was the other's fault that the creature had appeared. It was hunting someone named 'Quinn'.

His thoughts were again interrupted, but this time it was a soft moan from behind him. He had been standing before the door with his head down, lost in his own thoughts, and hadn't noticed when his companion had begun to come to. He turned around to find him struggling to sit up.

"We mustn't dally here," Ezra protested weakly.

"Ezra, my friend, you aren't in any shape to continue."

The other shook his head in denial as he swung his legs over the edge of the table. As Jonesy approached, he reached forward and snatched his left hand with a show of agility the latter hadn't expected. Turning his hand over, Ezra tapped the scar in the center of the palm before continuing.

"Do you believe you can use this on your own? Have I not given you 'His' strength through 'His' symbol each time that it was needed?"

Each time Ezra referenced the source of the cross's power, he rapped his knuckles on the scar.

"Listen to me, Lachlan. This isn't up to you, or me, any longer. I am but the vessel, while you are the bearer of his faith. I have known since meeting you that it would take the both of us to do that which is needed, but what I didn't realize is that there has to be another."

"The girl," Jonesy breathed. His thoughts jumped back to when he stood outside of the car, moments after having sent the beast tumbling across the concrete. He had seen her crouching on the ledge of the second story, wearing nothing but a soaked hospital gown and a determined look on her face.

"An heir," the priest finished mysteriously. "We can only give him his life and his faith, but it has to be someone special who can return to him his love. Without the three, we are all doomed."

"How can you know all of this?"

"It is not important, how, but why. Help me down. Let us find the girl before it is too late."

Jonesy helped the elderly priest from the desk, steadying him when he swayed unsteadily on his feet.

He approached the door, again listening for any sign of danger outside before opening it. When he was confident that it was safe, he slowly turned the handle. To the left, across the intersection they hand first

173

entered to get to this room, one of the elevators dinged
as it opened.

Before he could step into the hallway, Ezra grabbed
onto the duster from behind and stopped him. The door
was partially open, not enough for him to peek his head
out and look around, but it allowed the chilling sounds
of what had come from the elevator to reach them.

scriiip-smack, scriiip-smack

It was accompanied by the sound of labored breathing,
the kind you would expect from someone who had just
sprinted several hundred feet. It continued to approach
for several minutes, seemingly heading straight for
them, and he turned to his friend with a pleading look.
Again, the latter only shook his head.

Just when he thought he could take it no longer, the
sound began to fade. Whatever had come off of the
elevator was now moving in a direction away from where
they were hiding. There was the sound of a door opening
further down the hall, and it wasn't until several
minutes after it had closed that Ezra nodded his
approval for them to continue.

No longer playing the lone gunslinger, Jonesy removed
Jessie from her holster, and after checking to make sure
that she was loaded, he pointed her barrel to the
ceiling and they resumed their trek to the elevators.

The first thing they saw was the three foot wide
trail of blood. Whatever had come off of the elevator
had been in bad shape and he knew that if it was still
alive, it wouldn't be for much longer. The trail led to
the intersection between the elevator and where they had
been holed up, turning only once toward the hall from
which they had originally come. There were bloody
handprints on both sides of the trail, and when they
looked down to the doors leading into the massacre,
there were bloody prints all the way up the door showing
the struggle it must have been getting it open.

They only paused long enough to solemnly note the
details, as Ezra signed the cross, before continuing to
the elevator that the crawler hadn't come from.

They were in luck. Not only was it waiting on their
floor, but the interior was clean. They stepped inside,
pressed the button to the next level, and thanked their

maker that the generators allowed for these elevators to run.

When the doors opened, they were greeted by a scene similar to the one on the first level. There was a large blood trail passing directly in front of their elevator, with bloody handprints on either side of it, leading to the one they hadn't used. A quick search revealed its source. Lying against the wall was the lower half of a person Jonesy suspected had crawled past their room. Whatever had gotten ahold of (him? her?) had torn the poor person completely in half.

"*God*," he thought as his stomach lurched sickeningly, "*how are we going to face whatever did* THAT?"

Just past the remains of the crawler was a door that had been ripped partially from its hinges. It hung outward, held to the door frame only by the bent remains of the bottom hinge, rocking slightly back and forth. If left alone; it would likely be still in another moment or two. The number on the door read 137.

"We must not be too far behind," Jonesy whispered.

"Do not forget what I told you in the car; it can only be killed by holy weapons, silver, or by complete incineration."

He still didn't see how the last was going to be possible, but he didn't argue. The first two were covered by the gun and crossbow, and he couldn't foresee a situation where the third was applicable without bringing down the entire building.

There was an earsplitting shriek from down the hall, feminine, and full of terror. The pitch of the scream became so high that his earns rang from the sound. Ezra nudged him from behind and it was all that he needed to get into action. With the latter holding onto the duster behind him, he began to quickly move into the face of danger.

The hall turned sharply to the left and they were within ten feet of the corner when a woman suddenly flew around it. It was the woman he had seen from the ledge, only now she was wearing blue jeans and a pink blouse. Her hair trailed out behind her as she rounded the corner, but she yet to see them.

It happened between two blinks of an eye. She was sliding around the corner, frantically motioning for someone behind her to follow. Because her attention was on whom, or whatever was behind her, she hadn't seen them. She spun, reaching to for an unseen person with both hands. It was then they finally closed the distance to her, and at that moment she let out a *yelp* of terror and jumped backwards.

A silver haired nurse suddenly flew into view. Unlike this woman's hurried flight, however, hers was completely authentic. Both of her feet were off of the ground. Before he could comprehend the angle at which she flew by, it was over. She slammed into the wall in front of them, but before she could slide so much as an inch toward the floor, a large desk slammed into her with enough force that it crushed her upper body into the wall. A large spray of blood, bone, and brain matter arced out from the point of impact, spraying all three to witness it.

"No, goddamn you, NO!"

The woman screamed down the hall at whatever had thrown the desk; defiantly taking a stand against a creature she had no hope of defeating.

Jonesy stepped in front of her and it was then that she saw him, if only from behind.

"Stay back," he ordered.

"John," she asked, confused. "MY John?"

Ezra placed his hand on her shoulder, further adding to her confusion when she turned and noticed that it wasn't Quinn.

"Who are you?"

"It's not important," the older man answered firmly. "What's important is that we take down this abomination and send it back to hell where it belongs!"

"Y-you're a priest," she exclaims when she sees the white square beneath his chin. He doesn't answer, however, as he removes a very familiar bible from inside of a black cloth.

No further conversation was possible at this point, because at that moment they were interrupted by yet another high pitched howl.

176

"Sweet Jesus," Jonesy cried as he looked upon the creature for the first time. The creature filled the entire hall, from its shoulders to the tips of its ear. Its fur was as white as snow, or rather, it would be if wasn't matted down by the blood of its victims. It had only one arm, the other was missing below the elbow, and a large swath of fur was missing from one side and part of its face. It was the albino, the Jackal, and it had come to take its prize.

Pinned by the tremendous muscles remaining in its bad arm was the unconscious form of someone the woman knew all too well. He was one of her best friends, the second to the last person she had seen before she had 'died', and he seemed to reach pathetically for her with arms that were encased in plaster.

"Oh my god, Quinn!" she cried. "Let him go you bastard!"

The creature snarled before it spoke. Its voice was eerily familiar to her, evoking memories of when she had last heard it in its human form. At the same time it was completely foreign, animalistic, and it rolled off the beast's tongue like thunder.

"The master desires this one alive. Nothing you can do, or say, will stop this from happening. Bare your neck to me, and I will be merciful. Resist and I will suck the eyes from your skulls."

"I shall fear no evil," Jonesy spoke as he bared the palm of his left hand to the creature. "Thou mocketh the Lord with your vile existence. Leave your victim and be gone, lest we send you chasing your screams straight back to the pit from which you came!"

Chloe saw through the illusion as soon as he spoke. This wasn't her John standing before the albino. This was an imposter! So many questions suddenly needed answered, but there was no time to ask them. A golden glow surrounded the hand of the imposter, pulsing to the beat of words spoken by the priest.

"The Lord is my shepherd, I shall not want," he read, translating the Latin prayer into English. "He maketh me lie down in green pastures…"

The Jackal laughed and the sound of its guttural voice echoed off the walls around them.

177

"Silly things! Your prayers will not work on me! I do not believe in your God!"

"Foolish creature, 'He' believeth in you," Jonesy shouted. Golden light shot from his hand, once again matching the design of the scar burned into it. While it did not have the same effect on this creature, as it had on the vampires before it, it was enough to force the Jackal to throw its good arm over its face in an effort to block out the blinding light.

"I will fear no evil: for thou art with me; thy rod and thy staff they comfort me!"

The golden cross continued to blind the eyes of the beast, just as Ezra continued to read the passage during the exchange. Jonesy wasted no more time as he drew Jessie from her holster, leveling the barrel at the monster's core. As he was pulled the trigger, Chloe leapt forward and knocked his arm down. The bullet smashed harmlessly into the ground at their feet, her interference had been enough to sabotage his bead on the target, and their ears rang from the effects of firing the gun in such closed quarters.

"It's got my friend," she screamed. "You could have hit him!"

It was completely illogical that she prevented his shot, but how could she have known that up until a few hours ago he had been a decorated officer of the law? The moment of confusion was all that the beast needed to set forth its course of action. As they struggled for control of his firearm, it turned and smashed through the wall to their right. A few seconds later, there was another crash as it smashed its way out of the building. Jonesy pushed Chloe roughly to the side and followed, but it was too late.

The others had caught up to him as he reached the opening to the outside. They stood shoulder to shoulder, framed by the hole that it had created during its exit, and watched helplessly as the creature and its victim vanished into the darkness below.

XV

FROM THE ASHES

The rain continued to fall outside, drumming its song against the sea of concrete in an age old symphony which would go unappreciated this night. Wisps of fog lifted off of the ground here and there, but not enough so as to cover the ground. Yellow lines marked the ground where cars could be left during visitation, but very few spaces were filled this night. Most of those occupied were near the front, where the hospital's staff could park and easily get inside to start their shift.

Closer to the front of the building, there were a few vehicles which had been recently smashed. The damage was sporadic, from one side of the parking lane to the other, and was caused by a driver who had been erratically swerving back and forth. At the end of the parking lane, and sitting partially in the lane parallel with the front of the building, is a severely damaged Impala. Part of the roof was torn away, the windows are busted out, and the passenger front tire is sitting on its rim.

At first glance, one might mistake this vehicle for having been in an accident, but there were signs of something more sinister that suggested otherwise. Long jagged grooves told the tale of how a monstrously clawed hand had shredded the steel, destroyed by some unimaginable creature as it fought to get at the vehicle's occupants. Similar grooves marred the hood of the car as well.

The lights in the hospital were out, save for the soft red glow of the emergency bulbs, and no activity was evident in or around the first floor. On the second floor, however, is a gaping hole, inside of which three figures can briefly be seen looking out moments before stepping back into the room behind them.

Chloe is the first to move, quickly placing several feet between herself, the priest, and the imposter. The priest turns with her, following her with his sunken eyes and hollow expression. The imposter continued to stare out into the storm, searching for some sign of the lycanthrope that had gotten away. Her critical gaze took in every detail as she studied this strange man who wore John's clothes.

His height and build are very similar to J.R.'s, and she could see how easy it was for her to mistake his identity like she did. The similarities ended there, however. Unlike her John, this one wore what had probably started the day as the polished boots of either someone in law enforcement, or else the military. She could also see the bottom of his dark blue slacks beneath the bottom of the duster.

He was slightly stooped over, which, to her, were signs of someone who was either carrying more weight than they were used to, or this person was much older than the man who usually wore the hunter's garments. He stood against the right side of the hole, leaning slightly on his right arm, which was resting against the edge of the opening. She saw, with no small measure of disdain, that Jessie was resting comfortably in the grip of his right hand.

He turned slowly towards the two and she was again struck with a strong feeling of déjà vu. John's hat was pulled down low over his eyes, effectively shadowing over all features above his lips. There were some wrinkles around the latter, but if one didn't know that this wasn't a trait shared by J.R., one also wouldn't know it wasn't J.R. whom they were looking at.

"We're running out of time," he spoke softly. His voice was raspy and tired. She notice a very small hint of an accent in his words, perhaps Irish, but it had been mostly worn away over the years. "I know you don't know who I am, but you have to trust me when I say; 'We have the same goals.'"

She looked from the imposter to the priest. The latter wore the dark cloth and white square signifying his station, but she thought it possible he had since retired from the duties associated them, long ago. He was way too advanced for very much physical activity at a time, let alone the strenuous night he must've had thus far, and it showed. His hands, which held J.R.'s trusty bible, shook, and his skin had grown pale from his exertions.

"Let us find him before it is too late," the priest wearily prompted.

"Too late," she asked in confusion.

As if to answer her question from somewhere nearby they heard the *fwoomp* of a fire as it burst into existence. They would never discover its source, nor would the fire marshals in future investigations, for it originated at the first point of entry the albino had made into the building. He had crashed into a server room for the hospital's computers, and an exposed wire had finally swung into a pile of papers, instantly combusting the dry material.

"Like he said," Reminded the imposter, "before it's too late."

Flames licked hungrily against the walls of the hospital, quickly transforming everything in its path into ash, or molten piles of liquid metal, the latter which promptly ate through whatever was around or beneath it. The three ran out into the hall, where, to the right of their room the fire angrily grew larger by the second.

"Son of a bitch," she muttered. "You would think that there was some kind of accelerant involved. How in the hell is it getting so hot, so fast?!"

"We're in the critical care ward, I'm sure there's plenty of oxygen being routed to each room for it to consume," answered the pseudo-John.

They turned and ran the other direction, past the crushed nurse and the pair of severed legs, beyond the elevators, to a door marked with the universal symbol for stairs.

"How are we going to get there if the elevators aren't working," the old priest gasped.

The man with no name turned and looked down at the priest with no small amount of compassion.

"We'll have to use the stairs, I'm afraid."

He reached out and patted the older man on the shoulder with his left hand, and it was then that Chloe noticed the scar covering his palm.

She opened her mouth to say something, but he had already turned to push the door open. Smoke bellowed out, quickly filling the hall with its evil dark

181

currents, and they jumped out if its way where they waited for it to thin enough to enter. When it did, the one who hid behind the visage of J.R. entered and looked over the railing.

"I don't think the fire is in here yet. It looks like something is blocking the door open on the first level. Let's go, but make sure your mouth is covered. The smoke looks thicker down there."

"Wait," she said as they entered the stairwell. "Give me second before we go down."

Before either could protest, she turned and ran to a room that she knew hadn't been occupied, and quickly entered. Without a second to spare, and with the others at her heels, she dashed to where the nurses kept the extra linens for the room, and paused to grab a pillow case.

"Here," she said as she tossed it to the imposter. "Why don't you show me how big those muscles are and tear me three strips from that, six inches wide and no less, big boy."

He caught on when she began filling up the washbasin in the bathroom, and within seconds had torn the three strips just as she had asked for. Without a moment's hesitation, she took and dipped each into the water before returning one to each of her companions. She mimed how to use them by wringing out some of the water, folding, and then, tying it around her mouth.

While they did the same, she brushed past them and returned to the stairwell. The makeshift masks didn't keep all of the smoke out, but it allowed her to breathe without choking. Hopefully it would buy them enough time to get to wherever they were going.

Her unknown rescuers returned and began descending the stairs while she stood there in thought, the priest stopping only long enough to tug the sleeve of her blouse and motion for her to follow. They were grateful for her ingenuity. While the masks were difficult to breathe through, without sucking in some of the water, they did keep a large amount of the smoke out of their lungs. It was slow going, it was hard to see through the smoke rolling over the lip of the open door, but they quickly found a rhythm that kept them moving.

The man in the hat would take a couple steps, followed by the priest, and then her guarding the rear. They had initially gone down two at a time, but halfway down the first flight were the remains of two people blocking the way forward. It was grisly work, but the big guy rolled one of the bodies out of the way and they were able to continue. From then on, they took it one stair at a time until they were out of the smoke.

When they finally reached floor level, they discovered that the door was being held open by a triangular wedge. Nobody argued when the imposter kicked the wedge out, allowing it to close. There was no way they were going to get very far on this level anyhow; the fire was now close enough that it had raised the temperature several degrees.

With the smoke effectively blocked back into the first floor, they removed their masks, now dry and useless, and tossed them to the side.

"What do we do now," the priest asked fearfully. "We're trapped!"

"Not necessarily. We can go down from here, but we're going to need a bit more luck on our side."

"What do you mean, luck," Chloe asked. "What's that got to do with anything?"

"Everything," the big guy answered solemnly. "Most of the basement level is password protected. I know the password for the door that we need to get to, but what I don't know is if it's the same password used everywhere else."

"Wait, what do you mean 'for the door that we need to get to'? Where is it, exactly, that we are going?"

"We're going to return these," he said, motioning to John's things, "to the person they belong to."

She nodded, accepting his answer because there it would get her closer to 'him'. A shiver of excitement danced through her at the thought of seeing her mentor, her lover, her John once again, and she followed them down the stairs with an extra bounce in her step. It had yet to occur to her to ask why they had to go to the basement of the hospital in order to get to him.

As they continued further down the stairs, they could hear the sounds which normally accompany a fire of such

the magnitude as the one above them. There was the
crackling of the fire itself, the occasional crash as
the building began to crumble into the flames and the
explosion of some contained chemical giving way to the
heat.

"Do you think anyone else got out," Chloe asked
quietly.

Her mysterious companions looked quickly to one
another, sharing a heavy secret in the silence between
them, before the priest answered in a voice that was
thick and unconvincing.

"Y-yeah. I'm sure that we're the only ones who are
still alive."

The subtext of his message passed completely over her
head as she breathed a sigh of relief. She didn't think
she would ever forget what that monster had done to that
nurse upstairs, and she wouldn't be able to live with
herself if there were others who could have been helped
along the way.

The man in the wide brimmed hat had continued on down
the few remaining steps, to the door on the basement
level, leaving them where they stood.

"Come my child," the priest said to her. "Even if
there were any other survivors, what chance would we
have of finding them now? We have to trust that they
were evacuated by the surviving staff, before the fire
became too dangerous."

"Yeah, I suppose you're right," she answered
grudgingly. "I'm just tired. There's been so much
needless death over these last few days and-"

"Shh… Come now. 'He' will see to 'his' flock. Right
now, we need to worry about ourselves."

She nodded and smiled, leaning forward to give him a
brief hug, which he returned warmly.

"It works," interrupted the other from below. There
was an accepting *buzz*, followed by a *click* as the
door's locking mechanism electronically released, and he
began to pull it open. "We had better hurry before the
generator gets cut off."

"Why, what happens then," she asked nervously.

"If we're still down here, we'll be trapped until either rescued from the outside, our air supply runs out, or worse."

"Well what are you waiting for, Tall, Dark and Mysterious? Lead on!"

She smiled, winking playfully as she bounded down the remaining stairs. The priest was seconds behind her as they entered the sterile room on the other side.

"What *is* this place?"

"I'm not sure," he replied. "It could be something for the burn ward, but I didn't think that it was down here. Maybe some kind of facility for testing, perhaps?"

The door to the stairwell clicked shut behind them as the lock slid back into place.

"Well, there's no going back now boys," she said with a mischievous grin. "How's about we quit yapping like a bunch of little schoolgirls, and find us a way out of here?"

The room was uninteresting to look at. All six sides of the interior were fitted with brilliant white tiles, making it nearly impossible to find where the doors were once they were closed. They spread out and began feeling along the three walls they had to choose from, looking for some sort of trigger mechanism or hidden panel.

The priest had the best luck of the three when he found what he thought was a door in the center of the wall and to the right of where they entered.

"Over here," he called out. "I think I found something."

They met him at the wall and verified that it was indeed a door, but it would be several minutes before they discovered the panel to the right of it. It opened only when the man in the hat leaned against the wall in exasperation. Just as the door to the outside had, there was small number pad with a screen above it, prompting the user to enter a password. With a smile, he entered the combination and pressed the Enter key.

"The password you have entered is incorrect. Warning! An incorrect password had been input into sector 4. Warning!"

"I'm thinking that this isn't the burn ward," Chloe muttered sarcastically.

"This isn't the way I usually come down here," the wielder of Jessie explained apologetically. "I've only ever used the elevator!"

The alarm continued to vocalize its disapproval over the intercom, warning anyone listening of their intrusion.

"Fuck this. Watch out there, big guy."

Chloe reached down to where she had strapped on a pistol she had earlier found in the hands of a dead security guard. Very much the type of weapon she was used to, she removed the Glock .22 and aimed it at the screen above the keypad, firing three rounds into the frowning face that had appeared there. There was the sound of air hissing as the door slid into the wall to their left. She smile and motioned for the man with the Cross-shaped scar to continue.

"How did you know that would open," he asked incredulously.

"I thought why not? It always works in the movies, right?"

He chuckled as he turned and led their small group into the hallway beyond. Directly to their left is a long glass window, approximately three foot high by ten foot in length. They aren't able to see behind it, the room on the other side is filled with dark, acrid smoke. There is a door at the far end of the window, but it is locked and there wasn't any way to open it from the outside, not that they would want to.

The hall continued on for several feet before ending at another similar to the one Chloe had hacked with her gun.

"Do you think the password will work," asked the old priest.

"I don't know. I think we should continue to use hers to open the doors. It seems to be quicker."

She nodded, stepped past him, and like before, she placed a bullet into the keypad. A shower of sparks erupted from the keypad and the door clicked open. This one swung inward a couple inches before stopping.

186

"Now you're getting the idea," she teased as she pushed it open and stepped into another hall.

The hallway ran to the right and left, the ends of which branched off in two directions on either side. They were closer to the intersection to their right, but the imposter turned left and began walking in a long strides. The priest had to jog to keep up, while she walked at a brisk pace at his side.

"I take it you know where we are now?"

Her heart beat faster from the thought of seeing the man she loved, more than it did from the physical toll that came of their situation. She knew that she shouldn't feel the way that she did. She also knew that he didn't feel the same way about her as she did about him. It was completely irrational, but it was also something she couldn't control, nor try to change. She had fallen in love with him the first time they met and she had carried that torch every day since. She lived for the time that they spent together, and she would gladly die for her beloved hunter of all things creepy.

"*My gawd, hun, you've already done it once*," she thought giddily. And indeed she had. If she hadn't looked away from her attackers, things might have turned out a lot differently than they had.

Their feet echoed off of the walls, the sound chasing them with its frantic pace as they turned corner after corner. They came across nobody, but then again, there wasn't any reason to believe that they would. The hospital was burning to the ground, over their heads, and it wouldn't be much longer before the coals began eating their way into where they were. Only a fool would stay down here for much longer.

Their pace unknowingly increased as they continued to follow the gunslinger, and soon they were sprinting through the halls. She was comfortable with the pace. She had run no less than three miles every day for the last twenty-five years, but her companions soon fell behind. It wasn't until she realized that the one who wasn't her John was no longer next to her, that she stopped and turned around.

They were twenty feet behind her. The man in John's hat was kneeling next to the priest, who had collapsed.

The bible had flown from his hand, as well as the black
cloth and the ribbon used to bind it together, and had
slid several feet away. The big guy had his hand on the
older man's left shoulder and was calling to him as she
jogged back to where they were.

"Ezra? Come on, please. Not now! Ezra!"

He rolled the man over and leaned forward, listening
for any sign that he was breathing.

"He's still breathing! Help me, please," he begged.
Something that John would never have done, she thought
abruptly. She then chastised herself for even thinking
such a callous thought. Kneeling on the other side of
the priest whom the imposter had named as Ezra, she took
his hand and felt for a pulse.

"It's weak, but it's there."

"His pills!" the other suddenly blurted. He began to
rifle through the older man's pockets until he came
across a small prescription bottle. She watched as he
popped the cap and shook one out before putting it to
the lips of the priest.

"He's not awake hun. You're gonna have to help him."

"How?!"

"Here, like this."

She leaned forward and gently opened his mouth,
allowing for the pill to slip inside. She closed his
mouth and then gently rubbed his neck as she tried to
coax his unconscious body into doing something that
normally happened as a reflex when something was trying
to go down. Finally, he swallowed the pill she'd tossed
to the back of his throat.

"How long does this usually take to work," she asked.

"I don't know. The last time was longer then the
first."

"You're gonna have to carry him then. It's not going
to be long before we're baked alive down here."

He nodded and carefully scooped him up. While he was
getting to his feet, she gently gathered up the bible
and it's bindings before turning back to other with a
quizzical expression on her face.

"Which way? I'll lead."

"It's not far now. Just down this hall, take a left
and it'll be the door at the end."

She walked past him as she followed the simple
directions he had given her. The mysterious stranger
had been carrying Ezra much as one would an infant,
cradling him gently in his arms and speaking softly to
him. She couldn't hear everything that he said, but
what she did chilled her to the bone.

"…I can't do this without you, old friend… I'm not
sure my faith is strong enough to wake him…"

She didn't stop to question him; instead, she
continued forward and turned the corner leading to their
destination. The hall was comparatively short, versus
the last dozen they had sprinted through, ending about
forty feet from where she stood. Her perception
radically changed, however, when she saw the sign on the
door.

All Saints - City Morgue

The hall began to stretch out before her, doubling,
tripling in length, until it seemed like it was now a
mile away.

"What is this," she breathed. "Why are we coming
here?"

"It is where we have to be. He waits for us in
there," the imposter said, motioning toward the door.

"John," she yelled questioningly. "John?!"

She took off at a sprint, running as if the all
demons of hell were on her heels. The door seemed to
get no closer, no matter how hard she pushed herself,
and for the first time since waking she felt truly
afraid.

Hot tears filled her eyes, obscuring her vision as
she ran. It wasn't true! Not her John! Not J.R. van
Helsing! He can't die! She felt her heart breaking,
not only at the thought of not only having lost the love
of her life, but for the idea that humanity had lost its
one true savior against the coming tides of darkness.

Before she knew it, the door was in front of her and
she turned her shoulder, crashing into it at full speed.
Unlike most of the doors they had come across, this one
was a wooden door that had been installed in a wooden
frame. When she slammed into it, the wood creaked and

gave beneath the impact, blasting open and sending her tumbling to the floor inside.

She came to rest on the floor between two steel tables, the kind that were specially designed for the special type of work that was to be done upon them. In front of her, the wall was made of several slide-out tables that, when closed, kept recent arrivals cold until ready for autopsy.

Her newest companions entered then, the other John still carrying Ezra as she was weakly getting back to her feet. The blow had stunned her, momentarily stolen her breath, but overall she was alright. The autopsy tables were empty, and a quick look around the room revealed there to be an office to the right of the door they had entered, as well as a walk-in cooler to the left, where bodies were stored until taken for burial.

"He has to be in one of those," said the man with no name as he laid Ezra onto one of the tables. "Sorry old friend, I know this isn't the ideal place to rest, but it will only be for a moment."

He walked over to one side of the wall and started looking at the tags on the outside of each compartment door, while she did the same from the other side.

"Wanna hear something fucked up," Chloe asked rhetorically. "I think I put a few of these down here."

"You're right, that is fucked up," he answered somberly. "If this were any day prior to the last, I might have put you away on that small confession."

She had been trying to get control of herself when she made that comment, but she was fighting a losing battle. She frantically started pulling the slabs open and unzipping each to see if one of them was the one she was looking for.

It was the imposter who found him, and she knew it by the sharp intake of breath he had taken. She was closing the slab she had been inspecting, when he began to unzip the bag in front of him. She recognized him almost immediately. It *was* John lying there before the imposter, cold and lifeless, his beautiful gold-grey orbs forever closed. His once tanned skin was now grey and pallid. There was no doubt about it, he was gone.

The bullet hole in his forehead was all the proof that she needed.

"Oh no," she sobbed. She tried to say something else, but the words choked in her throat.

She fell across his chest, trying to pull him to her as she buried her face against his neck. She wept uncontrollably, calling his name over and over for several minutes in the vain hope that the sound of her voice would bring him back to her. She did not see as the imposter began removing John's things and setting them neatly on the other table. Nor did she feel his touch as he gently removed the bible from between her and her love.

She was completely lost to the world around her just then. Nothing mattered at that moment, except for the feelings of betrayal that began to creep into her heart. She had been brought back from death for what? For this? This didn't make any sense! Why would Michael save her, only for her to find that John Rizzerio van Helsing, last of the Glorious Slayers and Savior to Humanity, was dead?!

As she battled her own internal struggle, another, more spiritual one, was taking place behind her. Ezra had somewhat returned to consciousness and was holding the bible in his lap while Jonesy gathered some things from J.R.'s satchel. His cross, on which the Christ appeared just as pale and lifeless as the one meant to wield it, a vial of holy water, and some images of friends and family were gathered together on the other autopsy table.

He stepped up beside her and gently placed his right hand onto her right shoulder while Ezra read from the book of the hunter.

"Hoc enim vobis dicimus in verbo Domini quianos qui vivimus qui residui sumus in adventum Domini non praeveniemus eos qui dormierunt."

A surge of power shot up Jonesy's arm and it felt as if it were burning him from the inside out. Golden light shot from his left hand and into the forehead of the man in front of him, causing the body to jump from the impact.

"Quoniam ipse Dominus in iussu et in voce archangeli et in tuba Dei descendet de caelo et mortui qui in Christo sunt resurgent primi."

Another pulse, more powerful than the first, burst forth from the center of his being. During the course of the reading, it felt as if his soul were coming undone, and he watched in a dreamlike state as the holy lightning shot from his arm and into the head of the hunter yet a second time. He faintly heard the woman pleading for him to stop, but it was out of his control. He was serving his purpose.

"Deinde nos qui vivimus qui relinquimur simul rapiemur cum illis in nubibus obviam Domino in aera et sic semper cum Domino erimus."

The priest, who had returned to his feet during the reading, stepped forward and set the bible above the head of the body, which was now beginning to twitch from the shocks it was receiving. He walked around to the other side and laid the cross in the center of the man's chest. Much like the body beneath it, the Christ had begun to writhe, as it, too, showed signs of life. Blood began to once more to seep from its wounds. Ezra opened the mouth of the Hunter and poured the holy water inside, closing it only when the vial was empty and finished the last of the words to his litany.

"Itaque consolamini invicem in verbis istis."

Jonesy groaned as he felt a final surge gathering inside of him. He felt weak, and his legs shook beneath him, threatening to send him tumbling to the ground before he could complete his task, but he had enough left to get the job down. *"Good ole Jonesy,"* he thought to himself wryly. *"You can always count on me to get the job done."*

His thoughts were instantly forgotten as the holy energy shot once more from the scar in his hand, entering the forehead of the man beneath it. There was a concussive blast that radiated out from the contact point, as the holy energy returned life into this body, which knocked the three companions from their feet. John's body, free of Chloe's grasp, fell back to the table where it began to dance the electrocution tango.

Jonesy was fading fast. The last twenty-four hours had taken more out of him than he had to begin with, and he was now paying the piper. As darkness closed in, he accepted the inevitable. He knew what was coming for him and he allowed it with a smile because one of the last thing's he saw was the golden glow spreading from John's eyes. It was so bright that it spread to a point nearly a foot in either direction of his head.

It was the only thing that kept the final darkness at bay, and it only did so for just a few short seconds, but when he finally let go, it was with the image of J.R. taking in one huge breath of air.

He succumbed to the darkness knowing that he had done what he was meant to do. He had fulfilled his purpose.

The Phoenix had risen.

"This is Alyssa Riviera, reporting to you live from All Saints General Mercy hospital for Channel 6 Action News. As you can see behind me, the entire southern end of the building has been consumed in flames. Members of the A.S.F.D. have been working hard to put out the fire for the last two hours, but so far little progress has been made.

Lieutenant Combs? Lieutenant Combs, can you please answer a few questions?"

"Yes ma'am, I'll do what I can."

"Do you have any idea what happened here tonight?"

"Unfortunately, we have very little to go on at this time. Until the fire has been contained, and the Fire Marshal deems it safe to enter, we can only speculate as to the cause."

"Witnesses have reported seeing three figures exiting the building just shortly before the fire department arrived. Do you have any idea who these people might have been?"

"No. Not at this time."

"There are also reports that there was some kind of attack shortly before the fire erupted. Do you think this has anything to do with the James Street Massacre?"

"There is currently no evidence to support this, no."

"Isn't it true that a survivor from the James Street Massacre was brought to this hospital?"

"No comment."

"Then would you care to comment on the rumor that what happened here might be due to a rogue officer from your department?"

"No comment. Now if you'll excuse me-"

"Well I can tell you one thing; this has been a very
scary situation down here. Police have roped off all
access to the hospital and nobody has been allowed to
enter the property since they arrived.
If you look over there, you can just see several
police officers as they search through a wrecked car. I
can't really tell what make or model it is from here,
but it looks as if the vehicle hit several other parked
cars before coming to a stop.
I'm really at a loss for words. You really don't
know how hot something like this is until you're right
next to it. Even from here, I'm breaking out in a
sweat. I can't imagine what it must be like for the men
and women who are working to get this under control."

"Okay, hold on a second-"

"This just in; breaking news as it appears that
officials from the local State Patrol have arrived on
the scene. Also, sources have indicated that the
A.S.P.D. has been taken over as a home base for the
State Patrol while they run their investigations. It
definitely appears that the James Street Massacre and
the Tragedy at All Saints Mercy are indeed connected.
Until we have more answers, we can only sit back,
watch, and pray that whatever is going on here comes to
a peaceful end."

Ecce non est auxilium mihi in me et necessarii quoque mei recesserunt a me
Behold there is no help for me in myself, and my familiar friends also are departed from me.

Et comedes fructum uteri tui et carnes filiorum et filiarum tuarum quas dedit tibi Dominus Deus tuus in angustia et vastitate qua opprimet te hostis tuus
And thou shalt eat the fruit of thy womb, and the flesh of thy sons and of thy daughters, which the Lord thy God shall give thee, in the distress and extremity wherewith thy enemy shall oppress thee.

Qui autem me audierit absque terrore requiescet et abundantia perfruetur malorum timore sublato
But he that shall hear me, shall rest without terror, and shall enjoy abundance, without fear of evils.

In lege Domini voluntas eius
the law of the Lord's will

Hoc enim vobis dicimus in verbo Domini quia nos qui vivimus qui residui sumus in adventum Domini non praeveniemus eos qui dormierunt
For this we say unto you in the word of the Lord, that we who are alive, who remain unto the coming of the Lord, shall not prevent them who have slept.

Quoniam ipse Dominus in iussu et in voce archangeli et in tuba Dei descendet de caelo et mortui qui in Christo sunt resurgent primi
For the Lord himself shall come down from heaven with commandment and with the voice of an archangel and with the trumpet of God: and the dead who are in Christ shall rise first.

Deinde nos qui vivimus qui relinquimur simul rapiemur cum illis in nubibus obviam Domino in aera et sic semper cum Domino erimus

Then we who are alive, who are left, shall be taken up together with them in the clouds to meet Christ, into the air: and so shall we be always with the Lord.

Itaque consolamini invicem in verbis istis
Wherefore, comfort ye one another with these words.

Thank you for reading my book. If you enjoy
my work, and would like to keep up with what
I'm doing, please like my Facebook page at;
https://www.facebook.com/RRichardsson
or follow me on Twitter @R_Richardsson today!

Please help me to continue writing by leaving
a review at Amazon.com, bn.com or any of my other eBook
distributors.

R. Richardsson, 2013

Coming Soon: J.R. van Helsing

www.ingramcontent.com/pod-product-compliance
Lightning Source LLC
Chambersburg PA
CBHW020115180626
46812CB00006B/2614